REMOVED FROM CIRCULATION

# ZAN HAGEN'S MARATHON

## *Also by R. R. Knudson*

ZANBALLER

JESUS SONG

YOU ARE THE RAIN

FOX RUNNING

ZANBANGER

ZANBOOMER

RINEHART LIFTS

SPEED

JUST ANOTHER LOVE STORY

F
Knu

# ZAN HAGEN'S
# MARATHON

## R. R. KNUDSON

*Farrar, Straus & Giroux*

NEW YORK

14000

*Text copyright © 1984 by R. R. Knudson*

Map on page 92 by Gary Everson, courtesy of
the Women's Marathon Trials Association and the
Capital City Marathon Association, copyright © 1983
Maps on pages 165 and 178 based on 1983 Avon
International Marathon map, courtesy of Avon Products, Inc.

*All rights reserved*

Library of Congress catalog card number: 84-47843

*Printed in the United States of America*

Published simultaneously in Canada by
Collins Publishers, Toronto

*Designed by Tere LoPrete*

FIRST EDITION, 1984

*For K. Switzer, in whose steps
every woman marathoner runs*

# ZAN HAGEN'S
# MARATHON

# 1

"Twenty-six miles is all."

Rinehart said that while he kept on walking ahead of Zan. She couldn't see his face but she knew that he was looking schemy, his eyes narrowed worse than Attila the Hun's sending barefoot troops up an Alp.

Zan glanced down at her orange Nikes. Even in running shoes her own feet felt safe from Rinehart's marathon. Yes, safe. *She'd never run it.* He could wave his earmuffs all he wanted, stamp his galoshes, seize her arm and squeeze it to convince her—she wasn't racing twenty-six miles. Never.

"Twenty-six miles, three hundred yards."

The numbers rolled sweetly off Rinehart's tongue. He made them sound like baby steps in a back-yard playpen. But Zan knew better: Rinehart was announcing her doom steps, all those miles he would have her run just because numbers about footracing fascinated him. They were his joy. Zan watched him wave his notebook, a sure sign he would scheme up a race still longer than twenty-six miles, three hundred yards.

"Twenty-six miles, three hundred and eighty-five yards, to be perfectly precise. Your official marathon distance."

Pure Rinehart! He had worked himself up to the wicked length of a race his best friend would have to run. Not him—not Arthur Rinehart's legs.

"Never, madman!" Zan shouted in his face.

Rinehart turned around to shoot Zan a look of instant death and waited for her to catch up. He straightened his glasses and smoothed his hair under his earmuffs. They walked side by side in silence until he asked, "Want me to carry your books or anything?"

"Listen, Rinehart, I'm not agreeing to run that many miles even if you carry *me* to school every day the rest of this year. So don't pretend to be Mr. Sweet Guy."

Rinehart shut up. For about a minute. "Three hundred yards—that's nothing to run. Only as far as we are from—see, way over there, that red-white-and-blue woman on Lee Highway."

"She's a mailbox, Rinehart. You better polish your glasses. Anyway, women don't dress like flags."

"They do in the Olympics."

Rinehart let that comment hang. He counted the last few feet by walking toe to heel toward the mailbox. Every foot he all but stepped out of his floppy galoshes. "There now. Three hundred yards isn't so far," he said, toeing the mailbox. "And to that white line ahead on the street is the final eighty-five yards. You can run it easily —and win."

Zan had to admit Rinehart could measure with his eyes. Sure he could. He was a scientist, the best in Robert E. Lee Junior-Senior High. He loved nothing better than pointing out, every day on their way to school, how this is an inch longer than that; this weighs more; this is more stable.

Hey, wait a minute. What a bamboozle! "Of course I can race your eighty-five final yards." Zan stopped in her tracks. "But where's that little extra detail about the twenty-six miles, pal?"

Rinehart took Zan's hand to coach her along to his finish line. Soothing words flew from his mouth.

"You're looking strong, Zanbaby." He squeezed her fingers gently.

"Let me walk in peace."

"YOUCANDOIT. YOUCANWIN."

"Don't drag me."

"You're out in front but a few other runners are still trying to nip you."

"Who?"

"A Russian, for one."

"Oh, gimme a break, Rinehart."

"Here comes Rumania. She's closing in on you."

"Never heard of Rumania. Where is it?"

"On your left."

Zan looked left before she thought, Ah, good grief. "I mean, where is the country, not the fake Rumania runner."

Rinehart paid no attention to Zan's geography question or to her reluctant feet. He pulled her faster toward his goal, the crosswalk in front of Lee High. The closer they came, the harder he urged her with his pretend announcer's voice: "We're here, ladies and gentlemen, at the summer Olympics in Los Angeles, covering the final eighty-five yards of the women's marathon. An American runner, Suzanne (Zan) Hagen from Arlington, Virginia, is in the lead. Not surprisingly. We reported to you earlier about her dedication as an athlete. Already in her sports career she's snared an MVP, helped the Lee team win a *Herald* tournament—"

"You're hurting my wrist, Rinehart. Hey, and don't forget my record last Friday at the Virginia Cross-Country. Please let go my hand."

"I take it back. Norway has the lead in this race. She's outlegging America bad."

"She's what? Never!"

"Ooops. Norway's fallen off. And Canada's fallen down. You're getting lucky, Zan."

"Ah, give those foreign runners a break."

"Ladies and gentlemen, you can forget about our

friendly neighbor Canada. She's stumbled over Brazil. It's still ZanAmerica in first, China second."

"Where did China come from all of a sudden?" Zan glanced over her shoulder.

"Zan first, China second. Zan gold, China silver. Now China's crimson uniform shoots past the U.S.A. It's Zan's last chance for the Olympic gold medal. She ignores her exploding lungs. She whizzes nearer the speedy Chinese girl until their elbows touch. They study each other from the corners of their eyes. Question: What is each girl thinking? Answer: Who will fail first, me or her?" Rinehart's voice rose to his top notes. "Hey, kick it, kick it, Zanbaby. Fluff off the Great Doll of China."

Zan shook away Rinehart's hand from hers and sprang for the crosswalk. She glanced over her shoulder again. No other country will beat us, she told her feet. She pounded along the pavement. She dropped her books, her lunchbag, her homework into slushy puddles. Now her arms pumped hard, upping her tempo until she ran recklessly.

Rinehart ambled along in her wake, yelling, "The Dragon Lady's fading. Stick it to her. Make her eat your dust and thunder." He picked up her world-history assignment, her Spanish papers—

"Eat that China," Zan said as her feet crossed Rinehart's Olympic scheme line. She slowed to a brisk walk, calling to him, "Your marathon felt like nothing. A marshmallow." From the school-bus turnaround she called, "Gold medal easy. I didn't even break a sweat."

Zan caught herself. "Ah, blast it, Rinehart, you wiggled me again." Embarrassed to death, she fled into the school building.

When he caught up with Zan at his locker, which was next to hers, Rinehart said, "Your face is chalk."

"Not from running any twenty-six miles, fellow. I'm white with rage." Both their lockers rumbled from a slam Zan gave her door. "Eighty-creeping-five yards," she grouched. "That distance—anyone could beat China." Going upstairs Zan promised herself no more finish-line fever. Never again.

"Here's your homework." Rinehart had wiped mud off with his scarf. "See you at lunch."

Zan muttered, "China, chop fooie."

## 2

Zan sprinted another eighty-five yards down the hall to homeroom because she had to be on time. She'd been late all through cross-country running season. Late to school, late home to dinner, late everywhere except to starting lines of her workouts and race.

"Present," she answered the roll. "No more Tardy City around here." Zan grinned at faces swiveled toward hers. "I'm done running," she said, then blew a kiss to her Nikes and sat down to smooth her drenched homework before the first-period bell. Rinehart had written and typed this history report. He often did her homework. In return she helped him with science experiments. She'd be his guinea pig again; he hadn't told her for what. She hadn't read his history report yet either.

Until now. Zan groaned as she read "The Exciting History of Certain Brilliant Marathon Races, from 490 B.C. in Ancient Greece until—" Her eyes shut in mid-title.

"Great title," E.J. whispered, leaning across the aisle to see why Zan was clutching her head and rocking from side to side. "And a catchy subject. But I thought your racing season ended yesterday."

"For everyone but Rinehart." Zan skimmed the water-logged sentences, pausing halfway down the page to ask E.J., "Whoever heard of such history? Arthur made it all up, sounds like. He invents history the exact same way he invents chemicals in his lab." At the end of page 1 Zan said, "I suppose he thinks I'll read this aloud in class and then dive straight out a window to the Olympic starting line."

"We're three thousand miles from the Los Angeles Olympics," E.J. said in her business-like voice. "Not even with the aid of Wizard Arthur Rinehart can you dive that far. Sample my report. It will calm you." E.J. handed Zan her own world-history paper. The crisp sheets covered with upright printing about "Albanian Sports" made Rinehart's marathon paper look like a mud pie.

Still, Zan felt happy to have any old forgery in case Mrs. Tunis called on her. Sure, Mrs. Tunis seemed like a nice lady in her old-fashioned way, but she had this vicious habit of asking kids to read from papers they'd neglected to write. She sniffed out clues no matter how deep kids looked her in the eyes when she asked, "Who will report first?"

Zan told E.J., "Okay, in history right off the bat I'll play like I don't have my homework." They were on their way to first period. "Tunis'll say, 'Ms. Hagen, I note you have misplaced your assignment,' and I'll say, 'Wrong.' I'll get to read aloud for the first time since last September. P.S., what's Albania?"

E.J. said, "A smallish country in Europe. You'll find out soon," and patted her homework paper.

Zan thought, Well, at least an Albanian's not breathing down my neck in a marathon.

"And I'll find out if you're really going to run a marathon." E.J. ducked into history class.

Zan ducked too, but she couldn't move past DumDum Cadden. He blocked the door with his arm, saying, "Let's us don't go in there, Hagen. Let's us cool our heels in the gym shooting baskets."

"You didn't do your homework?"

"Nope."

"Poor you," said Ruby Jean Twilly, easing under DumDum's arm.

Zan whispered, "Check this out, DumDum." She offered him page 2 of her report. "I'll go halvsies with you. Just write your name on top with mine and pretend we worked together at County Library. I'll pretend the same."

DumDum fingered the paper. "I dunno—it feels like some history of water." Nevertheless, he gave out with one huge grin as he plunked himself down at a front-row desk. "You can't beat this here history, Mrs. Tunis," he called, waving page 2 as much as it would wave.

"Bide your time, Mr. Cadden," suggested the tall woman at the blackboard.

"Yep, my report's a biggie. It's about—" DumDum squirmed around to find help from Zan.

"I'm sure your subject merits our attention." Mrs. Tunis finished glancing at her seating chart and marked an absentee slip. She opened a window. Then, with a warm smile for her students, she asked, "I wonder how many of you know that history was made last Friday by one of your classmates?"

"I declare," said Ruby Jean.

"Who?" asked everyone else.

Mrs. Tunis said, "Think about it."

Her infamous words brought moans from students. "Her and her 'think about it,' " whispered Ruby Jean.

"There never was a bigger waste than thinking," DumDum decided aloud.

Mrs. Tunis let that go. She erased the blackboard with long, slow strokes, saying, "Think." She shook off class guesses.

"Somebody in here had a car wreck?"

"Croaked?"

"Our kid started up a war?"

Mrs. Tunis said, "The history of teenagers includes positive events, you would do well to remember. Try to imagine opposites to your disasters." When forty eyes looked glazed with effort, she wrote a clue on the blackboard: "Contemporary history was made Friday, November 3, 1983, in our Virginia state capital, Richmond." She put the chalk firmly down.

Everyone copied her words mindlessly and waited for her announcement. Nothing in Mrs. Tunis's face gave her away. She wore her everyday pleasant expression. But if kids had noticed Zan right then, they might have gained their second clue. Her reddening face put it plainly. She'd done something to cause all that color. "I wish my face would do like hers," Zan murmured to E.J. "She hides what she's thinking."

"Well, first of all she thinks—and I know what." E.J. raised her hand.

"Aha, Ms. Johnston. Tell us who is our history maker." Mrs. Tunis retrieved her chalk. She trusted E.J. to come up with satisfactory answers.

E.J. said, "Zan Hagen won the Virginia Cross-Country Championship at Capital City Park in Richmond."

The class suddenly remembered reading this same news in *The Washington Herald*. Ruby Jean twirled her pen as she majorette-strutted clear across the room to present Zan with a pompom quickly made from Kleenex. DumDum Cadden raised a finger in the #1 position above Zan's head, while Lurleen Dewey, from a last-row desk, went "Gimme a Z" in her cheerleader screech before she had time to worry aloud, "Like, history isn't about playing, is it? I mean, history doesn't cover sports." Lurleen seemed deeply perplexed. "I mean, shouldn't Zan be a Roman or a Hun, ancient and all, and discover a foreign country?"

"She discovered a cross country, hohoho," DumDum said.

The class couldn't decide. Kids spoke up about admiring Zan, the sports hero of Robert E. Lee Junior-Senior High. They adored winners, make no mistake, but would Zan really take her place in a thick maroon history book like theirs? Or would she be their weekend homework assignment? Of course, the *Herald* sports page published her photo a lot. Did that really count for the future? Zan wasn't exactly Alexander the Great.

"She's only Zan the Perfect Athletic Machine," E.J. reminded everyone.

Mrs. Tunis let them argue. In fact, she encouraged a debate by writing further information on the blackboard. From a *Herald* clipping she copied, "Zan Hagen is Lee High's first long-distance runner of distinction. She ate up the three cross-country miles in fifteen minutes flat, a new course record." Mrs. Tunis regained control of the class with a keen glance and held up the *Herald*'s photograph of Zan. "I shall pass this around for you to see history being made," she said, handing the photo to DumDum. "Walter Cadden, what do you think?"

DumDum liked being called by his real name, so willingly he concentrated.

"Her eyes poke out. Lookit—she's drooling something terrible. Yuck."

"It's her gasping, you jerk. Lemme have that." Fritz Slappy snatched the photo. He studied Zan with respect.

"See how she's straining? Every muscle in her body stands out. Wow, what legs! You know that famous guy who runs and announces on TV, the one all legs and arms?"

E.J. said, "Frank Shorter. Zan holds her wrists the way Shorter holds his."

"I wish I was a blond," Ruby Jean Twilly concluded from the photo. "Zan's hair is styled to run in."

"Yeah, yeah, yeah," students agreed, even those not close enough to see the photograph.

Mrs. Tunis walked up and down rows of desks saying, "If we all say yes together and think alike, no one is thinking. And comparison with other athletes can be fruitful, but you must go further. Ms. Hagen is an individual—one of a kind, as are you all." She paused, offering the photograph to Zan herself. "At what point in your race did the *Herald* reporter take this?"

Zan was slipping down inch by inch in her seat. That and her red ears told a story of guilt. Okay, she felt pride about her championship race. But what got to her now was Mrs. Tunis. Just when Zan had plotted to read aloud a genuine Rinehart forgery, Old Lady Tunis had written

ZAN HAGEN: INDIVIDUAL IN HISTORY

on her world-history blackboard. What a neat thing to do! Zan hoped it wouldn't get erased before she could run out and set another record.

She had already collected dozens of photographs of

her sports self, and this one seemed identical. But to make up for trying to cheat Mrs. Tunis, Zan pored over the newspaper clipping.

She thought about herself.

She thought, I wish I was in color like on the cover of *People* magazine.

"I wish my race number hadn't slipped funny on my shirt. I should have pinned it better," Zan wished aloud. "I wish I weren't turning to look over my shoulder. Only scared runners look back." Zan asked the class, "Whose elbow is that in front of me?"

The class waited for Zan to supply her own answer. She thought about how tired she'd felt during the race. She closed her eyes. In her imagination she saw herself fighting to gain on Hyde. Once again she felt her hammering heart, her legs heavy as the Lincoln Memorial. The only parts of her that hadn't ached were her eyelashes. "I'll never race again," she whispered. She caught her breath and told Mrs. Tunis, "I suppose that's Hyde's elbow. Or Palmer Stearn's. So they had about two yards to go before—"

"Va-Voom!" Fritz interrupted. "You tore past like a shot."

"To tell you the truth, Mrs. Tunis, I felt like I'd run clear to China that race."

Mrs. Tunis asked, "And how did you feel when you won?"

Zan didn't waste a second. "I loved it."

"Which is common. *Winning has always been the first law of sports,* according to sports pages of newspapers," Mrs. Tunis wrote on the blackboard with cool deliberation. And underlined it. Kids wanted to know if this "newspaper" law should be copied into their notebooks along with their list of original Tunis laws.

"Like, it's a truer law than what you told us about just being Caesar doesn't make you right," reasoned Lurleen. As a varsity cheerleader she knew a truth or two. DumDum flipped through his class notes until he found another of Tunis's laws: *Thinking is harder than physical work.* He called out, "Nothing's harder than football, huh, Tunis?"

Zan didn't hear the answer. She stayed lost in her own photograph. She swore to herself she'd never again glance back over her shoulder in a race. She'd win without wondering where the other runners were behind her. She looked straight into Mrs. Tunis's eyes. "I'm thinking of running a marathon in the Olympics."

That popped like a grasshopper from Zan's mouth.

After the squealing and the hugs and the confetti that DumDum tore from paper Zan hoped wasn't page 2 of their report, Zan added, "My best friend, Arthur Rinehart, gave me the idea. He says I can demolish Russia and all of them. Get a gold medal."

"Gold's my favorite color," Ruby Jean sighed.

"If I train hard between now and Los Angeles," Zan added.

"California! Movie stars!" Double sighs from Ruby Jean.

More shrieks. And pats that Zan's shoulders didn't feel because already she felt the pain of all those hills to run. Why didn't they ever go down? Sitting there safe in world history, Zan winced. She wondered if runners from little countries like Gaul or Mesopotamia would have to run the same workouts she knew would start for her tomorrow at 6 a.m.—start unless Zan took back her Olympic-size brag. Mmm. Maybe if she changed the subject kids would forget the color of her medal. So she said, "To tell you the truth, Mrs. Tunis, Rinehart also helped me with—oh, what the heck—he wrote my whole history report to psych me up for the Olympic twenty-six miles."

There. Zan had said it. She'd confessed to forgery. Now for a trip to the principal's office.

"Then, Ms. Hagen, you shall begin today's oral reporting." Mrs. Tunis didn't mention flunking Zan in history. Her voice remained warm. She brought students to attention with a review of their assignment: to write about a favorite sport through the ages. "Mr. Rinehart and Ms. Hagen favor marathoning. So be it. Read on."

Kids settled back in their chairs, happy not to be reading first. Leave it to Hagen to entertain them. She usually did. On the basketball court. On the playing field. They could count on her for kicks. "We idolize you," some kids seemed to say with their eyes. Others seemed to urge, "Don't make a fool of yourself if you want to stay our star."

Zan read Rinehart's title: The Exciting History of Certain Brilliant Marathon Races, from 470 B.C. in

Ancient Greece until Suzanne Hagen's Victory for America in the Los Angeles Olympics." Zan stopped in disbelief.

"Victory? Mr. Rinehart is also a soothsayer?" asked Mrs. Tunis. "Read on."

Zan continued with Rinehart's first paragraph:

In ancient times the whole country of Persia decided to invade and plunder the small city of Athens in Greece. To this end, Persia landed soldiers at Marathon, a village northwest of Athens. The Athenian general marched his troops down to Marathon, and after a hard-fought battle defeated the Persians. Legends about this war tell us that a tired foot soldier, Pheidippides, was selected to run back to Athens with news of the victory.

There's that word again, Zan thought.

Pheidippides ran the distance in full battle armor without even stopping for a drink. The legends don't say how fast he ran. Once he arrived in Athens, he burst into the senate building and proclaimed, 'Hail! We are victorious.' Those were Pheidippides's last words on earth. He dropped dead of happiness and exhaustion.

Zan's breath failed her. She quit reading while "Oh no's" rippled along rows of desks. "Running killed the sucker," she heard Fritz exclaim. Ruby Jean asked Zan, "Wouldn't you just die if that happened to you in L.A.?"

Yes, Zan thought without thinking. But dying's better than losing. "Moving right along—" Zan sounded cheery but she wasn't all that happy about old Pheidippides's running to death.

When the modern Olympics began in 1896, Greek officials included a footrace from Marathon to Athens. The winner would receive these prizes: two thousand pounds of chocolate, a million drachmas, free shaves for life, a gold medal, and an olive wreath. Twenty-five competitors entered and ran along the legendary route taken by Pheidippides thousands of years earlier. A Greek goatherder, Spiridon Louis, won this first Olympic marathon in two hours, fifty-eight minutes and fifty seconds.

"Who croaked at the finish line that time?" Fritz asked.

Zan saw that Fritz and Lurleen were taking notes on her report and that DumDum had begun to inspect page 2 with some interest. Part of her brain converted the two hours and fifty-eight minutes into seven minutes per mile, and she suddenly felt better about marathoning. She could run a mile in well under five minutes. Easy. If only she'd been alive in 1896 she would have beaten Spiridon to all those Snickers bars. She'd ask Rinehart at lunch later what "drachmas" could be. For now she kept reading.

Spectators at the Olympics have witnessed a bit of cheating during marathons since 1896. For instance, a frontrunner in the 1908 race, Dorando Pietri from Italy, collapsed exhausted near the finish line. Olympic rules clearly state that no runner shall receive assistance; nevertheless, Pietri was revived by doctors and officials and helped on his way to first place. Later that same day, the Olympic Committee voted to disqualify him. They gave the gold instead to John Hayes, an *American*.

Whooping and whistling for America broke out in the class, so loud that Zan had to stop reading again. She liked the sound of kids cheering for her American teammate, but apparently Mrs. Tunis wasn't as impressed by Hayes because she said sharply, "I would hardly call such aid 'cheating.' What do you think prompted people to revive Signore Pietri that day long ago?"

"Like, they didn't know any better?" asked Lurleen.

Mrs. Tunis glanced at the ceiling, then said, "Kindness. Human kindness and compassion should be held as portions of the Olympic ideal, not simply winning or struggling to win." She stepped to the board and wrote HUMANITY not far from Zan's name. Lurleen uncapped her felt tip, expecting a Tunis law or lecture, but instead Mrs. Tunis told Zan to continue reading.

Zan said, "I'm skipping a paragraph about some Argentina guy named Zabala winning at the first Los Angeles Olympics in 1932. I'll read this neat part about Hitler."

Fritz yelled, "I hope he croaks at the starting gun."

It was the final day of the Berlin Olympics in 1936. Adolf Hitler lurked in a box seat covered with swastikas. He expected a German winner, to whom he would present an olive branch of peace. Imagine Adolf's disappointment when a Korean runner named Kitei Son became the first Olympic marathoner to cover the course inside two and a half hours.

Hmm—Zan calculated rapidly, just the way Rinehart had taught her: divide the twenty-six miles into the total minutes, in this case 150 minutes. She grinned at the result. She could have beaten Japan's Son and told Hitler to stuff his olive branch.

"Eat your heart out, Hitler," Zan concluded. She returned to her desk, having finished page 1.

Mrs. Tunis pronounced herself pleased so far with Arthur Rinehart's report and quite impressed when Walter Cadden volunteered to read page 2. She said, "Students, kindly notice if and when that olive branch appears again in any race. Peace might well be another Olympic ideal. Proceed, Mr. Cadden."

Peace, Zan thought.

So it's peaceful sitting here, not like tomorrow this same time when I'll be far from comfortable after my morning workout. Leg cramps aren't peaceful. Peace won't lead me to a gold medal. And that goes double for kindness, whatever Mrs. Tunis says. Kindness doesn't win races. Legs and arms win. Iron willpower wins, and surprise tactics figured out by Coach Rinehart.

Anyway, DumDum wasn't reading about olives. Instead, he stuttered on countries Zan had never heard of. After a while his voice became only a background for Zan. Cooped up at her desk, she could imagine herself racing in California. She'd never been West, but she knew about the Pacific coastal mountains from movies. They seemed about the height of Virginia's Shenandoahs. "Look out, hamstring muscles," Zan whispered to her calves. "Up. Up."

"There has never been a women's marathon at the Olympics," DumDum read, crashing into Zan's dream. He glanced from the report to all the puzzled faces before him. Including Zan's red face! He fumbled the next sentence.

"Women have run no Olympic races longer than 1,500—I mean one-five-oh-oh meters. How far's that?"

"Fifteen hundred meters is about a mile," Zan answered to cover up feeling tricked by Rinehart. She wouldn't be going to California after all. Oh, the pain.

DumDum continued: "Olympic officials from around the world have always believed that women are too fra-gile to run twenty-six miles."

"I could run a marathon before breakfast any day," Zan bragged. What else could she say?

Lurleen told Zan, " 'Course you could. We'll show those officials."

"Won't have to," Fritz yelled. He'd grabbed the report from DumDum and scanned it. Jumping to his feet he read the final paragraph. "At Los Angeles for the first time in world history women will be allowed to run an Olympic marathon. Each country is entitled to send three women to the starting line. No doubt the great Grete Waitz will be running for Norway. Forget her! Suzanne Hagen will go down in record books for her memorable achievement for the U.S."

"Whew! Boyohboy." Fritz had to dry his forehead.

Zan leaned back and clasped her hands behind her head, elbows out like wings. She imagined the best part of her race—fans waving American flags along *her* Olympic course. She heard "Long live Hagen" as she broke the finish string, and right after that she saw her photograph—in 3-D—on every Wheaties box in America.

# 3

Radiant smiles from her former teammates met Zan at lunch that same day. News of her Olympic gold medal had spread faster than if she'd run shouting through the halls of Robert E. Lee High herself.

"Sit by me, Zanner," offered Aileen Dickerson. "Have a Twinkie."

"All the way. We got extra helpings," called Eugene Matello from the basketball training table.

Zan dodged her friends and their goodies. She made for her usual private table in a corner of the cafeteria, where her closest pals had already gathered.

DEFIANCE JUNIOR HIGH LIBRARY

"Hey, guys," she said to Rinehart and Monk Cunningham. "What a swell report you gave on Albanian sports, E.J. I liked about Eastern Europe's speed secrets."

Zan's damp brown-bag lunch was swept aside by Rinehart. He clapped his hands, pretending to summon a waiter. "Nothing's too costly for our heroine." Monk produced a plastic bag from under his zippered windbreaker. He doled out four fat hero sandwiches. Rinehart told Zan, "Today and today only you'll eat this junk food."

Monk proposed a solemn toast: "To Numero Uno. May she run forever." He held his sandwich high, pinching it so the bologna wouldn't fall out. "We have faith in you, Gold Hagen."

"And here's the champagne." Rinehart forked over four cans of ginger ale. He snapped them open so they fizzed down everyone's chin with the first sip. Soft yellow cheese stuck in their teeth. A feast, no less.

E.J. said, "This morning in history Walter didn't mention details of the Munich Olympics, when Frank Shorter drank seven gins after his win."

"How'd you know that?" Zan asked.

"I studied marathoning third period in the library. Shorter's race was brutal. Heat, humidity, and cobblestones. No wonder he resorted to alcohol afterward."

"Did you catch his winning time?" Zan asked.

Rinehart answered, "Two hours, twelve minutes, nineteen seconds. He ran five-minute miles."

Zan didn't blink. "I can run fives."

"The most you've run is three five-minute miles in a row. Frank Shorter ran twenty-six fives without stopping."

Zan still didn't blink at Rinehart. "I'll do it." She remembered E.J.'s oral history report, the part about some Eastern European women being banned from international competition because they used illegal drugs to help them run faster. She wondered aloud if United States drugstores sold the same medicine and if she could get away with popping a pill to speed twenty-six miles.

"Sample our dessert instead," E.J. offered. Rinehart opened his briefcase to show off a collection of sports candy bars: Baby Ruths, Reggies, Power Houses. Cheeks flushed with pride, Rinehart predicted a candy bar would be named for Zan after next summer. "The Hershey Company proudly presents 'Zanblitzer,' the first candy to celebrate a girl athlete."

Monk said, "Won't be made of gooey nougat, believe me."

"More like chocolate-covered nails," Zan said. She sat there basking in her friends' compliments. E.J. volunteered to raise money for Zan's airplane ticket to the trials next May 12 in Olympia, Washington. "We'll hold a bake sale. We'll sell Rae Ann Tupper's great fudge."

"What trials?" Zan hadn't been listening to that part of Rinehart's report.

Rinehart pulled out a notebook he always carried in his hip pocket: Rinehart's Log. He opened to a clean page and wrote something. He said, "Olympic trials.

That's how the United States chooses its team. Women run a trial marathon. The first-, second- and third-place finishers become our U.S. team. They go on to Los Angeles three months later for the Olympics."

Zan didn't miss a bite of her Power House. "Who'll finish second and third behind me?"

Rinehart held up his Log. "Most probably these two women will beat you. We're talking about third place for you at your stage of development next May when the trials are held."

"Third? Oh no," E.J. whispered.

Monk said, "Numero Threeo would still put you in Los Angeles." He chewed nervously on his St. Christopher medal.

Zan didn't glance at the names in Rinehart's Log. "Beat me? no way!" she said, and that was that. She tuned out and watched Mrs. Tunis passing through the lunch line with Lee High's principal. When her tray was full, Mrs. Tunis moved toward Zan's table in the corner.

"I suspected I would catch Mr. Rinehart here to thank him for his well-worded report," she said in her agreeable way.

"My pleasure, ma'am," Rinehart answered.

No further sound came from their table. This gang of four wasn't used to partying with a teacher present. Mrs. Tunis, trying to draw them out, said they reminded her of delegates in a United Nations meeting, so serious they were. She straightened Monk's black windbreaker on the back of his chair. She asked if she might help Zan to achieve her goals as a runner. In the silence that followed she was about to leave for the teachers' dining room when Zan mentioned, "Coach Rinehart here predicts I'll be third at the trials next May. But I know I'll be first, don't you, Mrs. Tunis?"

"Indeed I don't. I allow as how I have little knowledge of sports except what I've learned from students' homework over the years. I've not been athletic. You might gather that reading is my only active sport."

"Active—you kidding me?" This question slipped out before Zan could stop it. She clapped a hand over her mouth, hoping Mrs. Tunis wouldn't flunk her.

Monk feverishly bit his medal. But again Mrs. Tunis eased tension. "I meant *mentally* active. The mind must be quick—agile—balanced—strong—coordinated." She chose these words in her unhurried way. "In short, the mind must be 'athletic' in order to think creatively—to generate ideas not had by anyone before." She set down her lunch tray and laid a cool hand on Zan's head. "One can almost picture a mind at work. Beneath hair. Beneath bone. Ms. Hagen, your mind is working now. It's running."

Zan felt thumping under her short blond hair.

"Your mind's running because you've fed it lunch for energy; you've fed it information all morning in classes. I would hope you've left it open and flexible as it runs."

This running image was so vivid that Zan saw her mind in a race against her legs. Naturally her legs were winning. Her mind lagged. "Faster," she warned. "Catch up." Zan frowned in confusion. "I want my mind to sprint, not lope," she said to impress Mrs. Tunis.

The rest of the party laughed, making Zan flush.

Hey, what the heck. She was a superstar. Stars were to be worshipped, not to be messed over in front of an okay teacher. Zan boasted, "You should see my finishing kick, Mrs. Tunis. I'm better at kicking than at knowing about foreign countries."

"It seems so." Mrs. Tunis consulted a small watch pinned to her dress. "May I join you for lunch?" When no one objected and Monk stood to pull out her chair, she sat down before her tray. "I would be pleased to attend one of Ms. Hagen's races. When and where, Mr. Rinehart?"

"Tomorrow soon enough?" Zan babbled.

Rinehart said, "You'll do no such thing," to Zan; then to Mrs. Tunis he said, "She must run one marathon before next May. She needs to qualify for the trials. But her aerobic system won't be ready for several months."

Mrs. Tunis's salad fork stopped in midair. "She isn't qualified? I scarcely believe that."

"Olympic rules, ma'am. Women are allowed in the U.S. trials next May only if they've already done a marathon in two hours, fifty-one minutes, sixteen seconds."

"Is that beyond you, Ms. Hagen?"

"I could run six-minute miles with my legs tied together in a gunny sack."

"When and where?" asked Zan's by-now-favorite teacher.

"Want to taste some of my champagne—I mean soda, Mrs. Tunis? I maybe could find a marathon to run this coming Saturday or next. I'll check out the *Herald* sports page." Zan felt eager to qualify now that she'd heard the word.

But Rinehart had other ideas. Zan needed to build up her distance during the coming three months. "I'm recommending she run one hundred miles a week."

"Aw, Rinehart."

"And change her diet."

"I'll swallow those Albanian pills. I'll drink gin like Shorter."

But no way could she make the qualifying time before early next March. "Zan'll qualify then, leaving her two months afterward to recuperate for the trials in May and two months again to come back for the Olympic Marathon in August." Rinehart closed his Log and waited for Zan's accepting grin.

E.J. said, "Great future." Monk folded his hands in approval. Mrs. Tunis patted her mouth with a paper napkin and rose to leave the party, which wasn't festive any longer. Zan sulked madly, grumbling, "Who needs you guys? Lurleen, DumDum, Eugene Matello, and them would give anything to be with me on the road this Saturday in a race. My second-best friends aren't as wimpy as you. Our principal, too. Mr. Manfred knows some glory for Lee High School when he sniffs it. He'll drive me to a starting line anywhere in America in his school station wagon. Bet you."

"He means well," Rinehart stated between his teeth. That was Rinehart's absolute worst criticism.

Now Zan grouched at Rinehart, "You yourself mean well with the distant fame you've cooked up for me. Hey, I'm into instant history-making." Zan stood up tall. She hollered to Lurleen Dewey across the cafeteria, "Me, me. Sing a fight song for my first step to a qualifying time this coming Saturday."

"What first step?"

"Watch me."

Zan ran from table to table, tagging kids. "I'm gold next summer," she told the school. Kids from her home-room replied with the Lee fight song, except that Lurleen changed the words to

> HAGEN will shine tonight.
> HAGEN will shine,
> HAGEN will shine tonight,
> All down the line.
> She's all dressed up tonight.
> That's one good sign.
> When the sun goes down
> And the moon comes up,
> HAGEN WILL SHINE!

Zan roared past Rinehart, grabbing his Log. She stopped short to find the names he'd written of runners who would beat her in the trials. "Are you kidding? Who's this Julie Brown? Joan Benoit? Who could they be faster than me?" Zan was so psyched up she demanded of Mrs. Tunis, "Come see me Saturday in my first marathon ever. At the finish line I'll dunk my winning olives in my gin."

Mrs. Tunis allowed as how "time will tell."

# 4

The Robert E. Lee station wagon rode like a U-Haul. Zan tried to sleep but couldn't in the bumps and sways on Interstate 85. She felt crowded between DumDum and Lurleen in the back seat and disturbed by the dippy comments of Mr. Manfred. He talked fast, drove slow. Zan had to wonder if she'd reach the starting line by noon. But that was the least of her worries. Behind her, in the jump seat, Ronald Mergler, Jr., of the *Herald* loaded his cameras, rewound his tape recorder, and scribbled notes from the hypes Mr. Manfred fed him. Zan worried that she couldn't live up to Manfred's inflated promises to the *Herald*, that she couldn't even *finish* the 26-mile race.

She worried because she realized how much she didn't know about long-distance running. Since dumping her coach and team of best friends, she'd had ten days to ask around Arlington County about qualifying. About training. About a marathon to run. She'd finally found one posted on the bulletin board of Clarendon Sports Store: Tri-State Marathon, November 17, in Durham, North Carolina. Way down South. A 250-mile drive from Lee High. That's five hours of listening to Mr. Manfred spout comments like "Our very own little Miss Suzanne Hagen has this sporting caper in the bag."

And Lurleen reply, "You got that right, Prince."

DumDum snored.

And Mrs. Tunis read a map aloud to help her principal find his way South.

Durham was big. Zan forced herself to look out the window to see whether the racecourse might be—oh, please be, she hoped—level. But hills loomed here and there. Runners warmed up on the hills. Many of the women runners seemed to know one another well enough to hug and kiss at a sign-up table that the station wagon eventually neared.

REGISTER HERE FOR THE TRI-STATE MARATHON read a sign.

"Stop quick," Zan commanded. She skimmed over the sleeping DumDum and jumped into the waiting line. At the table she borrowed a pencil for filling out an entry form about her age, sex, and affiliation. "Robert E. Lee High," Zan wrote, then scratched that out to put "U.S.A." She'd let these home folks know she'd be representing every state in America next August in California. She exchanged her entry form for a paper number and pinned it to her orange racing shirt.

Zan warmed up by jogging only as far as the ratty old station wagon. She took off her sweats, asking, "Hills? Distance? So what?" She couldn't let her race crew know she was worried about the next two hours and fifty-one minutes she planned to be on the streets of Durham.

Heck, she'd show more speed than that. Heck, she wouldn't just qualify—she'd set a record for Ronald Mergler's wide-angle lenses.

His camera caught Zan giving orders to Lurleen about where she should be waiting on the racecourse. Zan barked, "Stand at the 6-mile mark. You're my own personal cheerleader. While you're at it, cheer for the other runners passing by you. Cheer D-R-O-P D-E-A-D."

"Why are they all shaking hands?" Lurleen pointed to the starting line. "Aren't they out to, like, whup each other?"

Zan said, "They're flaky. You won't catch me psyching up any other runners. Why give enemies encouragement? DumDum, you be waiting at the halfway point to cheer me.

"Half of what?"

"Runners to your marks," hollered a man into a microphone. He unholstered a gun.

Zan hurried toward the crowd. She called back to

Mr. Manfred, "I'll see you in nineteen miles. I might need a drink by then, so hand me a Pepsi."

"Wonderful, Suzanne." He hadn't yet left the wheel of the station wagon.

Mrs. Tunis followed Zan to the starting line. She seemed to be enjoying today's holiday mood. She greeted runners with "Bon voyage." She told Zan, "I shall be hoping for your success. If I were your peer as an athlete, I should offer you some parting advice."

"See you in the finishers' chute," Zan answered, pushing herself into a front row of runners. Before the gun went off, she thought she heard, "Think." But it was probably "stink," because people around her were already sweating from their warm-ups.

After the gun she heard no friend until Lurleen.

Zan went into the race plan she'd cooked up while waiting for the gun to fire. "Surge out with the leaders," she instructed herself. "Let them pull you along. And smile like a winner for the press truck."

Four young college guys and Zan made up the lead pack. Ahead, maybe a hundred feet, was the press truck. It held journalists, photographers, and a TV cameraman on its flatbed. It moved at the same speed as the pack. All equipment pointed back at the race leaders. Zan tried to look super good for that TV camera, her first performance on the tube. She held her form perfectly except when she was straightening her paper number or brushing her hair from her still-dry forehead. She was so intent on impressing the daytime viewers that she missed hearing the time called as she went through the mile mark with a guy in a Duke jersey to her right and a guy from the University of South Carolina to her left. Just local colleges, Zan knew from TV basketball. My uniform will say "U.S.A." in L.A.

A mile. I feel fine, Zan thought.

The Duke guy must not be feeling so fine, Zan noticed, because he dropped from her side. Another runner took his place. Three abreast and two guys slightly behind them, this pack held its pace through the second mile. Zan saw the marker on a curb as they started up a slight hill. She smiled at the hill's height, nothing to match Sure-Kill Hill, that monster she'd run up in her championship three-mile race.

Zan felt no pain. Heck, why not give the TV cameraman a wink. And pick up the pace. Say "So long" to these college twirps. If she ran *alone* in front, the cameras would have no other choice than to focus on her orange shoes, shorts, and shirt, which would all be changing from pumpkin color to red, white, and blue next summer.

"So long slowpokes."

Downhill now, Zan stuck it to the pack. She flew. Front-running had never been this much fun for her. If Monk and E.J. were watching TV, they'd be proud they used to be her friends. They'd believe they could stop phoning her with scraps of advice about racing, passed on from Rinehart, who hadn't phoned. As for

Rinehart himself, he never watched daytime TV, but he might see her instant replay on *Network News Tonight*. Zan quickened her pace.

She was first.

Daylight second.

Mile 4.

Zan didn't believe she'd seen the 4-mile marker. Her legs felt like ten miles. Her lungs felt like twenty. Her eyes were so full of sweat that she'd read the marker wrong, okay? "What's the distance?" she called ahead to the press truck. Ronald Mergler, Jr., was a blur.

"We can't help y'all during this here race" came an unknown voice shooting back at Zan like a pistol.

Who needs help, Zan thought. She planned to run to the edge of death. By herself. Alone. With no help from a bunch of officials in three-piece suits. Or from this runner passing her. "You'll pay for going out like a fool," he warned and disappeared around a corner of downtown Durham.

Rooters lined the street. "Lordy, a girl in third place," Zan heard from the sidewalk.

Third? Only one runner passed me. Ooops, here's another, Zan noticed when she wasn't watching herself in shop windows. Her form looked ragged. Her left shoulder was lower than her right, her right wrist and arm swung wide from her body, twisting her slightly on the run. These flaws in form were slowing Zan down.

Form. Concentrate on form so it will improve, Zan urged herself silently. Her throat and lips were too dry for words. Far, far ahead she could see a table spread with paper cups. Runners stopped for drinks, tons of runners. How had they passed her in the few blocks she'd been walking to catch her breath? Near the refreshment table one runner was doubled over, his hands on his hips. Uh-oh—*her* hands on *her* hips, Zan saw, drawing closer to the table at the 5-mile mark.

Zan breezed by the table without grabbing for a paper cup.

Zanbreezer.

Breezed? Are you kidding? She pretended to breeze in order to psych out the thirsty runners. Zan flashed them some speed. She controlled her choky breathing. She corrected her arm carriage, body lean, and foot placement—for all of thirty yards. Then she fell apart. Too late for the drink she needed to replace oceans she'd sweated these first five miles!

Only five miles? Zan felt she'd already run from Marathon to Athens.

She slowed to a trot. She stopped to retie a shoelace. She jogged a half mile. She stopped to take off one shoe and straighten her lumpy sock. She turned her back on the parade of marathoners. Heck, let the saps run from here to oblivion. She didn't care.

"Gimme a Z," Zan heard in the distance.

"Hagen will, like, shine tonight.

"Hagen, everyone's passing you." Lurleen's voice sounded snippy.

"I'll overtake them later," Zan puffed. She'd finally made it to the 6-mile mark. Lurleen sat waiting in the shade of a holly tree.

"Stomp on 'em, you follow what I'm saying, Zan?"

That cheer helped Zan lift her feet and put them down for another mile and a mile beyond that. Like a zombie she moved two more miles to the 10-mile water station. Zan leaned on the table as she drank one cup after another. She didn't even know what she was drinking.

"Y'all right, girlie?" A man filling cups peered closely at Zan.

"Never better." What else could she say?

"Maybe y'all should be waiting here for help." He came around an ice chest toward Zan. "I'll be glad to call ya'll a doctor."

Zan sprinted away. "I'm qualifying or spitting blood trying," she warned the runners in her path. She scuffed through a hundred yards of discarded paper cups. She decided she'd run as far as where DumDum waited and let him hold her up while she emptied a pebble from her shoe. Would taking DumDum's help be cheating? she wondered vaguely on the run. If she sat down she might never stand up again.

Thirteen miles and no DumDum.

Thirteen miles, 192½ yards, and no DumDum.

Zan had reached the halfway point in her qualifying marathon.

"One hour, twelve minutes," called a man with an official's ribbon on his coat. He held a stopwatch. "One hour, twelve minutes, five seconds," he hollered to Zan's back. How fast would she need to go the second half of this race in order to make the qualifying time? Zan had to think hard about it with all these distractions. Spectators along the course were squirting hoses at the runners to cool them and offering glasses of iced tea.

Zan struggled to think during mile 14. All she came up with was, My knees hurt.

My lungs hurt.

My hangnails hurt.

My brain hurts too bad to substract one hour, twelve minutes from two hours, fifty-one minutes, Zan thought, stopping near a driveway. She dragged her foot through the gravel, drawing numbers.

$$\begin{array}{r} 251 \\ -112 \\ \hline 139 \end{array}$$

She had one hour and thirty-nine minutes to run the next thirteen miles. Take off, Zan coached herself. She'd need to run $7\frac{1}{2}$-minute miles, a laughably slow pace for her in a shorter race than this one. If only Zan could find strength to laugh—and finish today.

"Ho ho ho ho." DumDum had plenty of laughs, standing there at mile 14. He fell in step with Zan. "Hagen, your nose is running faster than your legs."

"I'm burnt out," Zan confessed.

"Let's us go around these ladies."

Zan answered with an abrupt stop to empty her shoes, then her socks of imaginary gravel. She ran her index finger between her toes. "DumDum, how many women went by you while you were waiting for me?"

"I dunno. I can't tell apart these skinny types. Yep, they wear the same hair and uniforms as each other."

Shoes on and re-retied, Zan left the curb with Dum-Dum. They chugged a mile together, an easy mile for Zan because DumDum recited knock-knock jokes to keep her mind off her leg cramps.

But new pain was busy elsewhere on Zan, she discovered when DumDum dropped out. He'd had it. She'd had it, too. Her shoulders were raw from her rubbing bra straps. Her mouth was a desert. Zan yearned for the Pepsi waiting at mile 19 with Manfred. She hoped that he wouldn't be too obvious about handing it to her. She couldn't face being disqualified after pain, pain, every step she took toward her goal.

The press truck was long gone. Zan couldn't use it as a psych-up.

So many women had passed Zan she had no chance for a runner-up trophy. Another reward gone for fighting her way to the top of this hill.

"And face it, Zanblooper, you won't make the qualifying time if you walk much farther," Zan had breath to tell herself.

For the first time in her running career she was walking *down* a hill. She paused to read the 18-mile marker. Why couldn't it say "26" instead? Zan wiped her face on her shirt, leaving more sweat in her eyes than before. "Forget it, Olympics," she said without shedding a tear. To heck with beating China. All Zan wanted was her frosty Pepsi and a ride home to bed forever.

What if she were to lie down and roll the hill? That would be a faster way to Manfred. But he'd faint at the sight of an orange wave washing toward his Buster Brown shoes, and then Zan would have to carry him to the parking lot instead of vice versa.

Anyway, he wasn't waiting at mile 19.

Zan shaded her eyes and gazed into the sunny afternoon. No nutsy fruitcake in any direction, she decided. A guy selling popsicles from a wagon beckoned her to buy. "You think I carry a purse in a race?" Zan asked him at the very moment she spied an empty Pepsi can in the gutter. She kicked it onto the racecourse. She kicked it one hundred yards of jogging before she sank down to rest under a magnolia on a Durham lawn. She crawled to lean against its trunk.

She hated crawling.

She hated marathoning.

She fell asleep hating the Olympic Committee for allowing women a marathon of their own in Los Angeles. She woke up hating Rinehart for teasing her into qualifying, hating Mrs. Tunis for leaving her to freeze here. Zan felt a stabbing stiffness in her joints. She crawled toward the street to lie there and wait for an ambulance to take pity on her.

"Come join us," called a fat lady waddling south on

the racecourse. "We'll pull you along." At her heels were little girls in Brownie dresses. They giggled at Zan's attempts to stand up.

Zan joined the Brownies. How else might she make it to the finishers' chute to meet Mrs. Tunis for a ride to the mortuary? Zan listened to chirpy little voices. "We're getting there," they said. The troop leader linked arms with Zan's tottering corpse. Zan hadn't strength to pull away. She hated sappy help, plus she'd get disqualified if the judges saw her being ushered to the heart of Durham.

"Four hours, twelve minutes, thirteen seconds." An official called the time at mile 21.

"I hate you," Zan replied. Oh, was it his dumb fault she'd been running hours and still hadn't finished the course?

Yes! Everyone shared the blame for her pain. The Nike Corporation for her shoes. The Moss Brown Company for her uniform. The mayor of Durham. Zan's kindergarten teacher for teaching her to race at recess. Mr. and Mrs. James K. Hagen for having Zanbaby in the first place. This idiotic circle of Brownies around her telling the story of Goldilocks just because they thought Zan's hair looked gold under the layers of salt and pine needles and, for all Zan knew, blood.

"What happened next?" Zan asked them. Their story kept her mind off the growing darkness. "Oh, please, what happened next?"

"We're here," said the troop leader. They all gathered

on a bus-stop bench. "Three miles multiplied by the nine of us is somewhat more than the total distance of a marathon," the leader explained in a voice ringing with pleasure.

How could Zan argue with such simpleminded logic? She was barely conscious. She drooped against the bus-stop bench. She let the Brownies kiss her goodbye even though she hated them. She hated the bus for carrying them away. She stood and staggered another mile. Then she ran with Pheidippides to mile 25. He'd come out of nowhere to help Zan along.

Pheidippides said "Hi" to her.

No, he said "Hail."

He said, "You are *not* victorious."

Zan heard him clearly. She saw him in his Greek soldier uniform looking like Alexander the Great in her history book. He brandished his sword for Zan to follow him into the final mile—and disappeared. Zan walked straight ahead. In her battle to stay conscious she chatted with other runners surrounding her. Spiridon Louis let Zan touch the Olympic gold medal swinging around his neck. Dorando Pietri swore he never once asked for help in the 1908 Olympics. Help was given to him over his fallen body and didn't count. He deserved the gold. He showed Zan how to keep herself running by watching the finish line.

With 385 yards left to run, Zan begged for a drink. She couldn't go on without it. She'd be a Did Not Finish in the *Herald*'s list of Tri-State marathoners.

She'd drink poison if it would pump her legs to the finishers' chute. She'd drink whatever liquid was in the cup Frank Shorter now tried to slip into her outstretched hand.

"Thanks," Zan told Mrs. Tunis, who was walking by her side the final eighty-five yards. Zan would willingly accept disqualification for this cup of water—this fresh comfort on a pitch-dark street in a city of strangers.

# 5

## SCHOOLGIRL LOSES
## BID TO QUALIFY
## FOR OLYMPIC TRIALS

Ronald Mergler, Jr.
*Herald* Staff Writer

*Durham, North Carolina, Nov. 17*—Suzanne Hagen of Arlington County, Virginia, competed here today in the tenth annual Tri-State Marathon. She failed in her attempt to run the 26-mile, 385 yard course in under 2 hours and 51 minutes, 16 seconds, a time that would have automatically sent her to the Olympic Marathon Trials next May 12th in Olympia, Washington.

Miss Hagen finished 1,438 in a field of 1,439. Her time was 6 hours flat.

The unusually warm weather for November brought wisteria into bloom along the streets of this fair city and proved a boon for local ice-cream salesmen. One veteran of the six previous Tri-States reported a record sales day. Interviewed at his empty wagon on the finish line, he confided his race plan had been KISS: Keep It Simple, Stupid. "I toted lemon popsicles, only flavor. More convenient than reaching every which way in a hurry. My customers appreciate the fast hands."

Winners were Jackson Greene, Danville, Virginia, in 2:20:18 and Mary Shea, North Carolina, in 2:36:9.

(Photo, p. 7c)

# 6

"It's the end of the world," Zan sobbed.

She lay on the dissecting table in Arthur Rinehart's laboratory. His lab filled the entire basement of the Rinehart house at 1714 Glebe Road.

"It's no such thing," he said without a hint of pity. "And you *are* in Ronald Mergler's photograph." Rinehart handed Zan his largest magnifying glass together with the crumpled photo she'd torn from the *Herald*'s sports page. "That's the back of your head. I'd recognize you anywhere."

Zan squinted through the glass. "The popsicle man's in perfect focus. Me, I'm a smudge."

"Useful photo, nonetheless. Specifically, you're not looking over your shoulder. I'll send this to the Chinese team for their bulletin board. Let them memorize your nape, your hairline, the shape of your skull. They'll see nothing else on the Olympic course but the back of your head. Only cowards show their faces to runners behind them."

Zan sobbed. She couldn't help it. She'd totaled herself yesterday, and today she'd come crawling to Rinehart begging, "Do something to take the pain away."

He'd disinfected and bandaged her blisters. He'd given her a massage. He'd picked seeds from his ferns and brewed her a cup of crud with them on his Bunsen burner. He'd allowed her to pat his tarantulas. His offer of a heart-lung transplant from a racehorse stood for any time Zan cared to be his experimental animal. He knew this horse out in Winchester, Virginia, that was absolutely pining to run in the Olympics.

But despite Rinehart's measures, gloom deepened in his laboratory. Hagen didn't shine today or yesterday. So what's to cause her to shine ever again? She moved from his dissecting table thinking it might be best to ease on out of Rinehart's scalpel range. Knowing him— eek—she might accidentally fall asleep here beside his test tubes and wake up on the starting line of the Kentucky Derby.

"Leg transplants," Zan grumbled. "Albanian pills would work better to make me fast."

"Training's the answer."

"For what?"

"For 104 days from today. Your qualifying race on March 1." Rinehart shuffled papers at his desk. Zan knew her training schedule was already written.

"I won't run without drugs. It's too painful—it's death."

"Your discomfort yesterday came from going out too fast, from not drinking at water stations, and from running without a race plan. From acting cute on a TV program that never left North Carolina. You hurt today from lack of training."

"No drugs, no more running," Zan repeated. When Rinehart didn't respond by reaching into his chest of chemicals, Zan tried to imagine her future without winning the Olympics.

She'd be an ordinary drip in history, not a full-page photograph in Mrs. Tunis's book.

Oh, the pain. Zan especially wanted to impress Mrs. Tunis because of how kind she'd been yesterday. Never mind showing off for Lurleen and DumDum: they'd giggled at Zan's next-to-last-place finish in Durham. But Mrs. Tunis had been tactful. She'd presumed the Durham course had caught Zan on an off day. She declared Zan a winner for being thoughtful enough to go against marathon rules and accept a drink exactly where the race director could see her coming toward the finish line.

Zan mentioned that paper cupful of water to Rinehart, the way the water tasted. "Like sipping an igloo," she said, and smacked her lips. "Mrs. Tunis's shoulder felt like a pillow."

"You're both wrong," Rinehart reminded Zan. "Mrs. Tunis for offering help, you for accepting it. The rule book forbids aid of any sort except drinks and sponges at the official stations."

"Why wasn't I disqualified?" Zan made the mistake of asking.

Rinehart hooted. "Why punish the next-to-last runner, who barely overtook an ice-cream vendor wheeling his cart the whole route?"

"I needed drugs. I need them now." Heck, she would inject any fluid that would boost her speed. Where were those spooky hypodermic needles? She was dying to be Frankenstein's marathoner.

Rows and rows of bottles lined the lab shelves. Dead newts in formaldehyde filled these, and dead snakes. They'd expired trying to beat Rinehart's stopwatch. On other shelves were training aids Rinehart had tried out on Zan during the cross-country season. The homemade arch supports had rotted in sweat. The reflective safety shirt gave Zan a rash. "Nice try," Zan had told him.

"Drugs!" Zan chanted. "Uggs-dray." She used pig Latin to sound like a foreign chemist. She paced around the equipment Rinehart had rigged to help her be a champion. She had trained with these barbells. She'd run on his treadmill.

"Your future teammate Joan Benoit wouldn't resort to chemicals," Rinehart said, to get this drug business out of the way.

"Let me beat her by using them."

"You know she's done 2:22:42 already to qualify for

the trials? A world-record time if we discount a 2:20 flat the wire services say was run in Canton."

"Best reason to pump me full of pills."

"I hear you," Rinehart said finally. He knew he would have to fill Zan in on his experiments eventually, or she'd dun him for drugs until the L.A. starting line.

Rinehart sat Zan down on a weight bench to listen. "These drugs the big-time athletes ingest. You can run up Arlington Boulevard and buy most of them at a People's Drugstore. For instance, plain aspirin relieves pain. Pain happens in races. Thus, aspirin seems to be helpful if taken before a race. Other athletes sniff those asthma inhalers you've seen on TV ads. Inhalers work to open up the bronchials so more of your air circulates. Also, there's stay-awake pills. They contain caffeine. Some athletes believe caffeine gives them extra energy. Prescription drugs like bennies seem to increase energy, according to some runners who also load up on mega-doses of vitamin pills. They actually believe strength comes from vitamins."

"Doesn't it?"

"Who knows? My mice didn't improve their speeds with injections of vitamins. On No Doz tablets they ran crooked. Aspirin put my gophers to sleep at the starting line. Frogs hopped well after a meal of Mars Bars but they exploded on Milky Ways. Same difference."

Zan looked around for the frog bits.

Rinehart wasn't finished. "After you've run your race

at the Olympics, your urine will be tested. If any of the banned drugs show up, you'll be disqualified."

"Is that how they caught the Albanians E.J. reported about?"

"Those women used steroids."

"Steroids cost much at Peoples Drugs?"

"They're on doctor's prescriptions. Very hard to get hold of. I got them—I won't tell you where."

"I'll ask our Lee team physician."

"He'll warn you."

"What of?" Zan didn't care what of. She'd be willing to turn purple to win.

"Hair," Rinehart said.

"Hair?"

"Women who take steroids grow stronger muscles to help them move faster, but they also grow beards."

"How would you know, Rinehart?" His face was pink and smooth.

"I read about steroids in *Science News*. When I made my own experiments—listen. My toads grew beards from taking light doses of steroids." Rinehart lifted down bottles of his former pets. Zan peered with a magnifying glass at toads he identified as females. They had whiskers, all right. One girl toad had a goatee.

"Shave her."

"Arthur Rinehart, a barber? I'm a parasurgeon. I don't operate on hair. Maybe I'd make an exception for you."

Rinehart stroked his chin, thinking. Zan stroked a

caged rabbit to get the feel of a beard. It might not be all that icky. "Zanbearder," she could go by. She remembered a girl in history class with a mustache. It must feel scratchy!

"A trade-off," Rinehart continued. "Beard for speed. But our way of getting speed is best: miles of training. This coming month you won't have time to watch *Sports Spectacular* or hang around with Monk, E.J.— anybody. Unless they train with you."

Zan wished plain old vitamins would give her an edge. But Rinehart had tested them with zero results. If he'd invented any safe pill, he'd let Zan in on it. He wanted her to win almost as much as she did after Durham. He already had her signed up for her qualifying race. He pulled a duplicate application from his Log. "I entered you as 'S. Hagen.' We'll lie low in this race."

"Where is it?"

"The course is flat. Sea level."

"Where?"

"Also ideal weather for racing. Likely to be forty-five degrees. The field of runners will be small. Local servicemen and women. No big names from the running community. Splits are called at the first mile and every five miles to help you with pacing. You'll find water stations every few miles. Cost of entering only three dollars. Cost of traveling—one metro ticket from Lee High." Rinehart looked at her. "Now you know."

"The United States Military Marathon," said Zan, unimpressed.

"Washington Monument to the Lincoln Memorial. Roundabout way."

"Big deal."

"That's just it. We don't want to star in the New York Marathon. We're unknown. Let's keep it that way. Let's barely make the qualifying time. Then when we appear at the starting line of the trials next May, no one will have heard of us. Famous runners won't key on us, use us as their rabbit. We'll creep out of the woodwork and catch the favorites by surprise."

"Who's this 'we' you mention? Are me and you running a three-legged race?" Zan felt growly. Obscurity wasn't her style. She'd prefer to be ZanBoston if her legs ever recovered from yesterday. Were they ever stiff!

But her memory hurt more. How could she look kids in the eyes at school after her disgraceful loss? "If me and you are 'we,' Rinehart, I get to blame half my loss in Durham on you, okay?"

"Fine."

"I'll explain how *your* race plan failed."

"Lovely." After many seasons of coaching Zan, Rinehart understood her moods and handled them expertly. He agreed with her when he needed to. Or said nothing. Or wiggled her into his way of doing things.

"Rinehart's race plan failed down South," Zan rehearsed.

He didn't correct her.

"Rinehart ordered me to sprint from the gun."

He smiled blandly.

Zan felt better. Now if she could fall asleep and not wake up until the first of March. She hated training. In the back of her mind she toyed with a tiny dose of steroids. "I'd grow sideburns. I could hide them under my regular hair."

Rinehart let that pass.

# 7

Zan is training this late afternoon with Monk and DumDum. Monk has a car. DumDum's learning to drive it. He's tooling up and down hills in Arlington National Cemetery, shining the lights for Zan to run in.

"It gets late early," says DumDum about the dusk. He's learning to drive and talk at the same time.

All these gravestones give Monk the willies. He sits in the back seat gnawing his St. Christopher medal and crossing himself. "Aren't there other hills in Arlington you can practice on besides here?"

"Not steeper,'" Zan pants into the car's open window. "Are you praying for me, Monk?"

"For fallen soldiers." Monk cringes at the twilit row of graves. "I'll pray for you, too."

"Prayers work best for runners who're fast," Zan assures Monk. The tearing sound of her breathing can be heard inside the car. Words come hard for her near the hilltop.

Zan's been convinced by Coach Rinehart that speed will be easier in a flat race if she trains on hills once a week. She's following his instructions, no questions asked. She's paying attention to her hill-running form. She's carrying her arms low. She's watching the highest point on the hill, not her shoes. "Shine the brights," she's been hounding DumDum. Zan accelerates now, over the hill's crest.

DumDum scratches his head. He's learning to drive one-handed. "I dunno about our soldier guys underground. How'd they all die, Hagen?"

"Killed in wars," Monk answers.

DumDum asks, "Who against?" In world history the class hasn't come to America yet.

"Us against Viet Nam, Korea, Germany, Japan, each other—" Monk shivers.

"U.S.A. against all different countries in the world." Zan helps DumDum on her trip downhill. She's controlling her pace to save lungs and legs for her next attack uphill. "The United States has fought on tons of continents."

DumDum guesses he must have been absent from history class the day Hagen learned that.

Zan doesn't mind telling him. "I read our whole textbook. I found a chapter to take over after my Olympics and a page for the photo of me winning a gold medal." Zan sprints ahead of the car.

Driving behind Zan, DumDum toots the horn and points to another row of grave markers. "Lookit. Too many got zapped. We musta lost," he figures out for himself.

Monk corrects DumDum. "America hasn't lost a war ever—yet."

"Coulda' fooled me," DumDum says, with his eyes on the crosses. He's driving and thinking at the same time.

Monk turns on the car stereo to scare ghosts away from Zan on her run uphill.


Zan's walking around the Robert E. Lee High track with Mrs. Tunis on their lunch hour. Naturally they're talking together. But don't worry. This is Zan's rest between sprint laps.

"I noticed you from my window, Ms. Hagen. The weather seems severe for you to be outside in your shorts and singlet."

Zan boasts, "I'm hot from scorching the track. Been running quarter-mile laps in less than sixty seconds each." Zan's not about to ask what a singlet is.

Mrs. Tunis says no more on the subject of weather. She walks along in her fur boots, two clonks to every one long stride of Zan's. She thanks Zan for letting her in on the mystery of a track's circumference. "One-fourth of a mile! I hadn't realized. Startling! My window view has never before invited me to investigate how far 'round my students run.'"

Impulsively Zan says, "I'm just that dumb. I can't find a place named C-A-N-T-O-N on the world map in your room. Rinehart isn't spilling the beans where.'"

"Will you be racing in Canton?"

"Coach Rinehart claims I'll go up against a girl from there at the Olympics. She's my own age but faster, if we can believe in news reports. She's been marathoning ever since she was eight years old. DumDum thinks Canton's someplace in New Jersey."

"Good for Walter. I daresay there's a Canton in most of our states. However, I would have presumed your coach has Canton, China, in mind."

Zan feels a chill with the word "China."

She resets her stopwatch to zero. "I'm sprinting another quarter. I'll pick you up again here."

From the starting line Zan shoots ahead in lane one. Her knees churn high. Her arm movement is directly forward and backward from the shoulders. That way her arms lead her legs. Her eyes are fixed ahead on the near turn, then to the back straightaway, then to the far turn, then to Mrs. Tunis at the finish line. "Fifty-seven seconds," Zan reports the time from her stopwatch.

"Upon my word, you've run a quarter mile closer to Canton. Such a friendly city. Your Cantonese opponent stands to be the same."

Zan catches her breath to ask, "Did you ever go to China?"

"Not in person. I've traveled there in books."

"Did you ever go to where the Olympics started up in Greece?"

"I'm afraid I've been only a few hundred miles, at the farthest, from Virginia. Were I not a reader I'd be largely untraveled. I've a good claim to being a stick-in-the-mud."

They are once more on Zan's starting line for another interval of sprinting. Zan keeps her mind from the coming chest pain by asking, "You remember those branches and wreaths of olives in my oral report? The olives people win for racing? Your books—do they explain why? Olives are cheapskaty instead of gold." Zan winds her stopwatch but waits for her teacher to answer.

Mrs. Tunis doesn't right away. She takes off a glove, puts it back on. "The olive, a native tree of Greece—oh, mercy—I trust I shall not blunder if I tell you truthfully that cuttings from such trees are quickly perishable." She holds a gloved hand toward Zan's stopwatch. "Might I keep your time this quarter mile? I fancy I'd learn from the experience."

Zan shows Mrs. Tunis how to stop and start the watch. "So what if olives rot?"

"Thus they symbolize the—the evanescence of victory."

Mrs. Tunis doesn't call "Think about it" as Zan breaks away from the starting line.


Zan's working out with Frank Shorter, Tom Hicks, and John Hayes, the only Americans ever to win Olympic marathons. These three are in Zan's mind, not in the pack; but to her they're as real as their gold medals she's read about. They brim with advice for Zan's long, slow, distance run this Saturday morning.

Frank Shorter says, "L.S.D.—long slow distance. Even if you feel fresh, make sure not to increase your speed above a jog."

Zan takes his advice. She jogs across the Potomac River on Chain Bridge, jogs down a ramp to the C & O Canal, jogs along the towpath.

"Observe closely the differing surfaces you run on," Tom Hicks cautions Zan. "Otherwise you may twist an ankle in footings of dust or mud. Many a cracked stone lies in wait to bring you down." Frank Shorter agrees about footing. He's been hobbled by cobblestones on the streets of Munich, Germany. He mentions his Olympic blisters, urging Zan to race in shoes that are well broken in yet not worn out. John Hayes warns Zan of patchy weeds along the canal.

Saturday runners crowd the C & O Canal towpath. Zan starts a kick to capture attention from them, but Hayes holds her back with a warning.

"Slow down. Following your 25-mile training plan today helps you follow your race plan later,'" he says. Tom Hicks tells Zan, "You must glide along here. Slowly glide like a barge."

"I'm a barge," Zan reminds herself for mile after mile along the canal. "Zanbarger."

Zanbarger for twenty miles. On her right side, the

canal water stands still. On her left side, runners pass her going away. In her mind, three U.S.A. Olympians review with her their golden races. Zan ought to know all about them by now; how Shorter won in Munich, Hayes in London, Hicks in St. Louis. Zan's been reading with E.J. at the Library of Congress when she isn't running. She's been reading to find out if victories are really effervescent.


Zan's climbing steps with Rinehart's voice in her ear. She's listening to a tape he made for her Walkman. He's coaching Zan by remote control, all the way from his lab in Arlington to the U.S. Capitol. He sent her there by metro to run the "marble hill"—one hundred Capitol steps, twenty times.

"Up," says Rinehart's voice on the tape.

"Where else?" Zan answers sarcastically.

"Up," says Rinehart. "Lift your knees."

"Thanks a lot."

"Up."

The tape isn't broken. It's as insistent as the beat of pop music's Top Ten.

"Up. Lift your arms with your knees. You're twenty-five steps from the top. Count along with me."

"I'm doing it, Coach."

"Steps are strengthening your legs. Strength is speed. Lift. You're soon to be a world champion."

"Ninety-eight, ninety-nine." Zan's been counting

steps. Arriving at the top, she quickly turns and hurries down the marble hill, two steps at a time. Her feet move in the rhythm of Rinehart's voice, which is singsonging about Zan's championship character.

"Zan, you're *self-confident.* You're *persistent.* You're *coachable.*"

Not always, she's thinking. I didn't listen to my coach about Durham, North Carolina.

The tape doesn't mention Zan's mistakes. "Turn around and run up, up, up, up. You enjoy confronting these steps for the sixteenth time this morning. You enjoy your own control over your legs, over your pain. You'll force yourself to run up. You're *determined.*"

"No one's here this early. Including you, Rinehart, home in your bed. Me at the U.S. Capitol. And I'm not even a tourist."

Zan turns off her Walkman. She spreads out on a cold marble bench. She rests her eyes on the Capitol's bronze doors, thinking that a big-cheese senator might appear. She'll tell him of Rinehart's race plan—to wage an all-out war against China. Zan'll ask her congressman why she can't get hold of steroids in a drugstore when some countries she can name train athletes on all kinds of banned dope. They'd already discovered how to fake their urine tests and everything. Rinehart says so. Shouldn't our U.S. at least get even for cheating?

To heck with senators! They're not in training. Just like her coach they're probably sleeping this morning.

Zan restarts her Walkman. She runs steps and listens.

"You're *mentally tough,* Zanbanger," Rinehart says

through the headphones. "You'll train when no one watches or helps. You're willing to endure physical pain."

"This is only my morning workout," Zan whispers. "The pain will be double tonight on Rinehart's treadmill."

"*Self-confidence. Drive. Coachability,*" Rinehart repeats.

Coachable? I'm a robot, Zan thinks. Rinehart's robot.


Zan's cruising along on Rinehart's treadmill, feeling no pain. His toasty warm laboratory is bright with surgical lights. A pan steams on his Bunsen burner, sending apple dumpling smells high and low. Two tables on either side of the treadmill are covered with small plastic bottles of cider.

"Reach for a drink with your right hand," Rinehart commands Zan.

Zan reaches to her right.

"Maintain your pace while you sip."

Zan sips on the run.

"When you've finished the bottle, drop it beside you. Don't toss it. You'll waste energy."

She lets the bottle slip to her side. She continues running, all smiles. That's because she loves apple cider. Also because there's no wind in Rinehart's lab. Windless air makes speed easier.

"Maintain your six-minute pace while you reach for a drink with your left hand."

Zan obeys by reaching, sipping.

"Drop your bottle. Keep your eyes on the treadmill —the road—for other bottles in your path. Runners ahead at your qualifying marathon will be littering the course."

"Swell reason for me to be front-runner," Zan says. But she knows she's wasting her voice because she's bound to follow Rinehart's strategy at the U.S. Military Marathon.

"Reach with your right hand . . . with your left hand . . . There's no detail too small to ignore during training. Don't lose time at any water station on the course."

"Only water?"

"There's water at all major marathons, both sides of the road. I'm using cider tonight to coax you into drinking practice." Rinehart opens his Log to write numbers on many pages.

Training Intensity pages. Environmental Factors pages. Training Volume pages. Rinehart holds the Log in front of Zan's eyes. He shows how she's reached his training goal of one hundred miles per week. He turns the page to Competitive Factors.

Zan spies a photo on that page along with numbers. She wants to know who it is.

"One billion people live in China," Rinehart whistles through his teeth. "This girl's the only one of them who worries me." He taps his glasses against the photo.

"Bring her over to the treadmill. I'll practice ignoring her."

Rinehart shakes his head. "First you make your qualifying time of 2:51:16 at the Military Marathon. Then I'll donate this picture to your locker door at school. You'll study your enemy between classes. She'll soon be as real to you as E.J., Lurleen, Ruby Jean, Aileen—"

"Who says I ever see friends since I've been training morning, noon, and night?"

"You've got me for your companion."

"Companion? Where were you this morning? Or last weekend when I ran L.S.D. to the White House and back. You could have pedaled your bike alongside me."

"I was riding it on the Military Marathon course, scheming up your race tactics."

"Pain's my only companion," Zan says, noticing now that her body is tiring, remembering how her thigh muscles ached yesterday after her golf-course run, her hamstrings flamed the day before on the Lee track, her calves the day before that on her run in Rock Creek Park.

One hundred miles a week, with pain her faithful companion.

Rinehart lifts the lid on a pan of steamed dumplings he's made Zan for energy. "Another mile and these are yours," he tempts her.


Zan's running downhill. It's her treat for training conscientiously the past months. Mrs. Tunis waits for her at the bottom of this long, gentle Blue Ridge Mountain in

Virginia. She's driven Zan to the top and she'll drive her safe home to Arlington again.

"Coast," Zan says to her legs. "Coast me to the bottom."

She's left to her own company.

What else is new?

"Float," she says, putting down one foot after another. She decides to dream about her Chinese enemy for the next miles.

After a while a sense of ease comes over Zan. She can turn her thoughts to Rinehart's qualifying-race plan. She'll be running *his* race this coming Sunday morning. He has already written her splits in indelible ink in the palms of her hands. She won't have to memorize his numbers. Just open her loosely cupped fingers and read.

She reads the numbers aloud, alone.

"A 6:15 first mile."

"At five miles, 31:22. Hit the ten-mile mark at 1:03:00 and the fifteen-mile mark at 1.35:00. I'll be slowing down gradually. At twenty miles I'll be 2:07:32. Looking tired but secretly feeling fresh, I hope. At twenty-five miles I'll be 2:41, with the final mile a 7:17. I'll barely qualify. No one will notice me."

Zan cups her hands again, back in perfect form.

No one will notice my form, she thinks. Soldiers passing won't see a slow girl in frayed gray sweats. Officials won't need to check my dawdling blood or urine for drugs. I'll be twenty-eight full minutes behind Joan

Benoit's world record and thirty minutes behind the time China claims as a world record for their girl.

Zan's mind and body are gliding, gliding down a Virginia mountain toward her Olympic trial qualifying time.

# 8

Boom.

The report of a small cannon started the United States Military Marathon.

Eight rows behind the wave of runners surging from the line, Zan moved slowly forward in a clump of U.S. Marines. Hips and elbows jostled her. Zan kept her form. Hadn't she practiced being squished by Eugene Matello and Fritz Slappy on the school track? Besides, she knew that these wasted seconds behind the starting line would be made up for in Rinehart's strategy. Zan remained hidden in the pack of Marines wearing camouflage T-shirts and shorts. She traveled in this "tank" along Constitution Avenue for the first mile.

"6:09," cried the timer over scattered cheers.

Zan compared her actual time to the first number written in her palm, then slowed a bit. The tank slowed around her. They all ran mechanically, wordlessly, reaching the 5-mile timer in

"31:15."

By now the distance was taking its toll. Several Marines fell behind, and others stopped dead around a corner, where a water station waited in ambush. Zan, who'd been expecting the table of paper cups, grabbed one, drank, dropped the empty, and ran on with a feeling of power held in check. A fair-sized crowd along The Mall responded to her sixth mile, seventh, eighth, with whistles, clapping, and not a few firecrackers. One voice called out to Zan, "You're the fifth-place woman."

"Fifth stinks," Zan said to herself. She could easily have been the first-place woman.

But she was right on Rinehart's schedule at the tenth mile in

"One hour, two minutes, forty-five seconds."

Rinehart would be proud of her. He'd be happy about her economical moves at the water station and delighted that she didn't wave at a low-flying helicopter just then. It might be loaded with reporters who weren't supposed to notice Zan's low-key race. She remembered the hood on her sweat shirt. In the finisher's chute she'd pull it up in a peak for a disguise.

The racecourse at this point circled past a statue of John Paul Jones and onto a road around the Tidal Basin. A sharp turn gave Zan the chance to use the technique

Rinehart had taught her from his research. Several strides before the turn she placed her body in a sideways position, outside shoulder forward, inside shoulder back; outside arm raised, inside arm down. Reaching the turn, Zan leaned and brought her legs into alignment with her shoulders. That way she "fell" around the turn, as Rinehart called it. Falling saved energy. Zan also saved steps by not going too wide on the turn.

Once out of it, Zan resumed her usual stance. She ran for a table and snatched a cup of water between the elbows of men resting there. Those who'd been ahead of her for fifteen miles were definitely slowing at

"1:34:02."

Race leaders were "coming back" to her, as Rinehart had predicted. Zan recognized a navy-blue singlet that she'd noticed in a front row of the starting line. It said, *Damn the torpedoes, full speed ahead.* She passed it without changing pace. With a stride costing little effort, she moved into a pack of T-shirts decorated with parachutes. Hey, these soldiers were alive, no doubt about that from their rasping along Independence Avenue. Zan hung with them for company until a voice hoarse from calling the times of faster runners told her pack:

"2:08:30."

Zan read the numbers in her palm, finding herself a full minute behind Rinehart's pace at the 20-mile marker. She'd need to speed up, leaving her company of servicemen, maybe joining another up ahead in the 6 miles and 385 yards left to run. But for now, break away.

With iron strength she owed to her training, Zan pumped her arms harder. They led her legs along The Mall again. She caught a woman runner. Zan almost said "Hi" but saved her breath. No point in perking up the competition. Zan said, "Beep beep," instead, and circled the Reflecting Pool. It showed her nothing because she wasn't looking anywhere except down at her feet or a few yards ahead at more racers coming back to her. And at wilted racers sitting on the grass. And at one lying in the course like an exhausted warrior. Zan wondered if he'd said "Hail" before falling. She was forced to jump over the guy in order to stick to Rinehart's pace.

"Two hours and forty seconds."

A band in the distance played "America." Zan ran for it. On a triple loop around the Air and Space Museum she reminded herself to hold back. She remembered to let her form go to pieces. She moaned in a tone she'd practiced on Rinehart's treadmill. For the final ten yards she alternated limping with walking.

"2:49:49."

Rinehart stood beside the chute with a blanket. He wrapped Zan up and whisked her away as soon as he was sure that her correct time and name had been recorded.

"You followed my plan to the last detail," he said later to the energetic jumping jack beside him on the metro home to Arlington. She'd hardly exhausted three months' worth of training strength. "You qualified," Rinehart reminded her.

"Bor-ing," said Zan.

# 9

The Olympics and only the Olympics were spoken of.

The biggest biggie. More fun than dying and going to heaven. Chartered buses to California for Zan's homeroom if kids could raise the money at a garage sale. No L.A. Coliseum ticket too costly for Mr. Manfred to witness Lee's wonderful "Princess Suzanne" defeat the world.

At school, friends were just sick they'd missed Zan's qualifying marathon. Why hadn't she told them? They wouldn't have cared how far behind the winners Zan had run. They loved her, anyway. They wouldn't have minded how early on Sunday morning she raced unless it was before they got up.

Monk Cunningham alone confessed he was glad he hadn't attended her race. "Those soldiers you ran around with spook me," he said. DumDum wanted Zan to explain to him the reason she didn't cream the whole U.S. Army after all her long training.

"Because I followed Rinehart's scheme," she said. "I held myself back. Racing's ninety percent mental."

"And the other half physical," DumDum figured out for himself.

The map in Mrs. Tunis's room suddenly had Christmas tree light bulbs sticking out from world capitals. "We shall light these bulbs as we read about women of other nations joining their teams," she announced to Zan's class while turning on the first bulb in Washington, D.C. "Ms. Hagen's name heads the list of Olympians we shall display on our bulletin board."

Zan didn't remind the class of one tiny detail: Olympic trials this coming May. She must get through the trial marathon in first, second, or third place to make the United States team. She'd mention the trials later on in the spring, if she ever had energy left from morning training.

All that was normal in Zan's teenage life disappeared. Rinehart's schedule called for a thousand miles to be run between her qualifying marathon and her May 12 trial in Olympia, Washington, leaving Zan no time for homework or for her jobs around the Hagen house. Or for movies, TV, telephone conversations. Or for reading the *Herald* sports page. Zan got up in the morning. She ran. She ate breakfast. Went to morning classes. Ate lunch when she wasn't doing speed work on the Lee track. Attended afternoon classes. Ran. Ate dinner. Slept. Got up. Ran.

"We're giving you a formal send-off parade like the Rose Bowl one. With Lee's band, a float, and all," said Ruby Jean Twilly one day.

"Feel free," Zan answered in her hurry from history class to Spanish.

"Can you ride a horse?"

"I'll ride the float."

"In an evening gown? Us majorettes'll be renting matching bridesmaid's dresses."

"Numero zero," Zan said to Monk about the dress. Her Spanish went no further than that.

Monk said, "I'm supposed to ask if you'll please donate a pair of your running shoes, autographed, to our sports auction? Fritz Slappy's giving his Dogwood Bowl trophy. E.J.'s autographing the game ball she won at the *Herald* basketball tournament. Every penny we make will send Mr. Manfred to Los Angeles."

"Tell you what, Monk. I'll let you have two pairs of my shoes, including the ones I qualified in, if the fruitcake will stay put in L.A. for good."

Friends caught Zan between classes or ran with her after. Otherwise she was gone. Fritz Slappy covered a mile with her to get in shape for the baseball season.

Lurleen Dewey sprinted one straightaway on Lee track with Zan to find out how a side stitch felt for a biology term paper. Ronald Mergler, Jr., nabbed Zan on her L.S.D. run past his office. He wanted an interview for the *Herald* but couldn't keep up with Zan for more than a block.

"Looking back on your Military Marathon—at what point did you feel positive you'd finish within the qualifying time?" Mr. Mergler asked.

"On the starting line."

"You raced that day unheeded by the media. Wearing a hooded sweatshirt was no way to garner your usual coverage."

"I'm turning here," Zan said to the tape recorder now bouncing around Mr. Mergler's neck.

"What's your strategy for the trials?" His voice was raspy with effort.

"I'll do my best."

"And the rest, as they say, will be history. Now tell me about—DRUGS," hollered Mr. Mergler down the block to Zan's back. "DOES ARTHUR RINEHART ADVOCATE THEIR USE?"

"Don't I wish."

Zan's answer didn't appear in the newspaper. Mr. Mergler's Sunday column completely bypassed the trials and dealt with her worldwide competition. He named countries he expected to contend for the medals and countries he suspected of training on steroids. He predicted the gold-medal marathon time: sub 2:20. He included wire-service photographs of three Albanian women in training. E.J. cut them out of his column for the world-history bulletin board.

"Great news. You're Ronald Mergler's dark horse," E.J. whispered to Zan as Mrs. Tunis lighted the lights in Albania, France, New Zealand, and Japan.

"Rinehart already told me. He wants to do a horse-heart transplant on me all the more." Zan thumped her chest.

Their whispers ceased with a question from Mrs. Tunis. "I wonder who knows why there are no lighted bulbs in this part of our world." She pointed to Central America.

Her students said as one person, "Think about it," before Mrs. Tunis prompted them.

She was the first to smile. She touched Guatemala, Honduras, and El Salvador with her fingertips. "Mr. Cadden, you appear to have an inkling why these countries may not be bound for the summer Olympics."

"Their guys are dead in war?"

Mrs. Tunis as well as DumDum looked pleased with his answer. "Indeed yes," she said. "Civil wars are preventing our neighbors to the south from using their financial resources and leisure time for athletics."

"Guns before sports," DumDum summed up for the class.

After class Zan asked him, "How'd you know?"

"I seen on TV. Wars before baseball, not the other way around on my set."

"I remember," Zan said.

Zan had no time to watch news or sports. Her days stretched from dawn to dark, with training the only thing on her mind. Rinehart wrote her homework papers, except world history, so Zan wouldn't cheat her favorite teacher. Rinehart tutored her for tests while she lifted weights in his lab. On weekends with no schoolwork to do, Zan's friends prepared for their own trips to L.A. Zan and her coach prepared for the trials.

Rinehart pored over a map of the racecourse that wound through the distant city of Olympia, Washington. He was able to concentrate even with Zan's dancing around his operating table. She was practicing a touchdown boogie she'd seen football players do in the end zone.

"How do you like it so far?" she asked Rinehart. It's the first end-zone spike on a marathon finish line."

"What will you spike?"

"My winner's olive wreath? No, that'll make it wilt even worse than time. Okay, I'll quick take off my shoes to spike. They'll bounce like a football."

Rinehart used his magnifying glass to study a humidity index, a tide table, a temperature chart, and a rainfall table for Olympia, Washington. He wrote figures in his Log. "It's bound to be our kind of weather out in the Northwest next month. Comfortable. Slightly misty if not drizzling. And our kind of course." He ran his felt tip along it.

Zan said, "Come on and help me decide if I want you

at the finish line to wrap me in a U.S. flag or waiting somewhere on the course to cheer me."

"I'll cheer long distance from my lab."

"Give me the map, Rinehart, and I'll mark a spot for you to be standing."

Without protest Rinehart slid the map across his operating table. Zan shut her eyes. "I love surprises. Just wait for me where I point to. You won't miss me even in my wishy-washy gray singlet. Can't miss the front-runner!"

Rinehart removed his glasses and cleaned them with surgical gauze. "You'll be in the second pack, maintaining contact with the leaders." Zan lay down on the weight bench. She said, "Boo, Benoit. Boo, Brown," instead of counting her bench presses.

"Our tactics are to hang back behind the two fastest runners, Joan and Julie. Allow them to pace you," Rinehart insisted.

Restored by her calm lifting rhythm, Zan could be reasoned with. She could be shown the pages of Rinehart's Log, the pages titled "Trials," and not want to shuffle past these to the Los Angeles tactics.

Ah. Tranquillity in Rinehart's lab.

Everywhere else in Arlington seethed with L.A. fever. Former Lee High sports hero Randy Boyle stole a day off from the New York Yankees to be auctioneer at the Olympics auction. He got big bucks for Rae Ann Tupper's Basepopcornballs and for Rinehart's collection of "Albanian" gerbils. Randy's own baseball cap brought enough money for the fruitcake's one-way ticket, so Randy tossed in his whole Yankee uniform for the round trip. Zan wasn't there to stop him. She wasn't in homeroom to help with the garage sale. Neither could she get together with Lee's cheerleaders to plan her throne on their float.

Zan's body went to her classes but most days her mind stayed on Rinehart's Log. She snuck time during lectures to stare at the trial-course map, to hypnotize herself with its turns. She wrote and then traced her pen over Rinehart's tactics when she was supposed to be listening.

Follow the leaders.
Stay close behind.
Stay on their pace.
At the right moment, overtake them into third place.

"Song Mai from Canton, China," Mrs. Tunis was lecturing one day toward the middle of April. She stood beside her world map. "Would you care to turn on her light bulb, Ms. Hagen?"

Lost in her trial in Olympia, Washington, Zan didn't hear.

Mrs. Tunis gave Zan a piercing look to restore her senses. "This will not do," she said about Zan's inattention. "Kindly help me find a bulb for China."

Zan fumbled up from her desk toward the map. She saw China, huge and crimson.

"Song Mai," Mrs. Tunis repeated. "From Canton. I

wish her well. Ms. Johnston clipped this photo of Ms. Song from *Sports* magazine."

E.J. came forward to tack the photo onto the bulletin board next to other women runners. "Song Mai—the People's Republic of China's gold-medal hopeful," E.J. read from the photo's caption. "She has never raced against Western women."

"Is China friendly or anything?" Lurleen asked Zan. "They're Communists and that. Is she one?"

"She's fast is all I care."

Mrs. Tunis used the remaining time to explain China's politics. Whatever they were, Zan couldn't bother about. Song Mai was just a girl her own age, her own height, it seemed from the photo. Wearing red, being "red," wasn't going to make Song Mai any faster.

Come to think of it, wearing red, white, and blue wasn't about to make Zan faster. And gray wouldn't hide her from these classmates if she blew first, second, or third place at the trials.

Zan's workouts got tougher. Spring days were longer and her friends eager to push her training so they'd be part of her golden future.

On the firm, wet shoreline at Virginia Beach, Zan ran an hour north, an hour south. Another afternoon she ran in the dry, soft beach dunes. That was beastly. Fifteen minutes and Zan's calf muscles stung with effort. She cooled them with fifteen minutes of high-knee runs in the ocean's shallows. DumDum waited in Fritz's truck. He was learning to park it and add numbers at the same time. When Zan repeated shortline sprints of 50, 100, 200, 400 yards, DumDum figured the numbers for her weekly total.

"Computer Cadden," Fritz nicknamed him.

Rinehart had to be sure that DumDum knew what he was computing about. Rinehart asked Zan every day when she brought her miles and speed to his laboratory.

"DumDum can chew gum, blow bubbles, and parallel park at the same time," Zan swore to her coach.

Rinehart held up an envelope. "And *I'm* able to get you a free airplane ticket from the trials committee. It finally came, along with your hotel reservations and your pre-race banquet ticket. A race official meets your flight and will drive you to the race site the next day."

"*Our* flight. Me. You."

"Only qualified runners travel free. As a coach I'd have to pay."

"Then cough up the money, Coach."

"Four hundred dollars? Spend that and I couldn't afford a ticket to see you in Los Angeles. As it is, I'll have to sell my lab equipment, my pets, my ferns—"

"I won't run alone by myself in a foreign state like Washington. My mom can't go. My dad, either, this time. Maybe with you for L.A."

"You're not alone in any race. Hundreds of other women—"

"Alone without you on the course. I need you."

"What for?"

"To help me."

"That's against the rules."

"To cheer for me."

"You wouldn't hear me over the other thousands."

"I'm not going."

"After all our training? You understand my race plan as well as I do. I couldn't run it more strategically myself."

"If you *could* run." Zan tossed herself down on Rinehart's operating table. "I'm not running in the trials."

Rinehart reached into his instrument tray and withdrew a scalpel.

"I'll go, I'll go! But on the starting line I'll tell the man to shoot me with his gun."

Rinehart uncorked a bottle of ether.

"Just kidding. I'll go if you'll give me some pain-killing pills to pop."

"A brain transplant is indicated," Rinehart said to Zan as if to an attending nurse.

Zan rolled off his table. "Okay, just for that I'll ask E.J. to go with me. She'll share my glory." When Rinehart said nothing, Zan left his lab and ran home down Glebe Road to phone E.J.

E.J. begged off the trials. "Great idea, but my grade point might dip if I cut school so close to finals."

Zan dialed DumDum.

Nope, he couldn't fly nowhere. He'd be driving that day, ho ho. He'd be at his driver's license test on the same date as her trial. May 12 was a biggie.

Zan didn't phone Monk Cunningham. Doubtless Monk planned to take DumDum to the Arlington Motor

Vehicle Bureau. And Fritz couldn't miss his job at the country club. "Sorry 'bout that. My truck payments you wouldn't believe."

Stuff your truck, Zan felt like saying. Plus stuff your Azalea Cotillion, Aileen Dickerson. If the phone hadn't rung just then, Zan might have been tempted to call Manfred for his company on her racecourse.

" 'Lo." She hoped it would be anybody who felt like flying West.

Rinehart said, "While you're goofing around *inside* your house, the woman who's going to beat you at the trials is *outside* running."

"Hang up, Rinehart. I'm calling Lurleen."

"She won't go. She'll be saving up for her Olympics in Disneyland."

"Okay, I'm calling Tunis. Teachers are rich. She'll fly out there."

Rinehart didn't disagree. Mrs. Tunis had been concerned and helpful during Zan's months of training. She hadn't attended Zan's qualifying marathon but that was only because she'd been "unwilling to favor military functions."

Rinehart advised Zan to go out and run her miles this evening before dark. "Wait and ask Mrs. Tunis tomorrow. You can also explain why you're racing twice on the West Coast. Does she understand trials?"

"I haven't reminded her. Kids in class, either. Nobody wants to turn off my light bulb on the map."

"Go run tonight. Run tomorrow morning. Tell Mrs. Tunis in person."

Zan's clear light bulb was still burning the next day in
world history. Zan herself unscrewed it from the map.
She didn't wait to be called on. She gave a lecture about
the trials. She wrote

2:50.14

on the blackboard. Staring at her feet she said, "This
qualifying time will put at least two hundred fifty U.S.
women on the starting line against me. You'll need more
light bulbs than the White House Christmas tree, Mrs.
Tunis."

"I dare say."

"Would you fly out to Olympia and twirl for me,
Ruby Jean? My coach can't afford the ticket." Zan
couldn't bring herself to ask Mrs. Tunis.

Ruby Jean said, "I'm busy organizing your L.A. send-
off parade."

"First things first, huh, Twilly?" DumDum's law.

Mrs. Tunis entered into Zan's trials with ready sym-
pathy. How fortunate Zan was to journey so far and so
often. How impressive to be able to race without Mr.
Rinehart at hand. "Ms. Hagen has a rare opportunity to
think for herself. She'll also make many new friends
among the other runners."

Are you out of your mind? Zan almost asked.

"Yep, Hagen can save them a piece of the finish tape,
ho ho."

"Let us suppose our Olympic team were to be selected according to the athletes' personal qualities. Thoughtfulness. Cooperation. Helpfulness—"

For the rest of that class period and for the remaining weeks before she flew to Olympia, Zan tried to imagine being pals with her racing enemies. Take Julie Brown. Four years ago Brown made the Olympic team as a miler. She could run a mile in 4:28. Multiply that by twenty-six miles and imagine the pain, not kindness, to come in the trials.

All the other women flying to Olympia could cooperate with Zan by snoozing in their Holiday Inn on the twelfth of May.

Heck, after the trials Song Mai could be internationally helpful by staying in Canton and tending her rice paddy.

The trials weren't mentioned again by kids at Lee High School. Only "L.A. CA." Their posters said, "From Va. to Ca." all over the halls. They screamed "ZanAngeles" up and down the cafeteria. The afternoon she left for National Airport in the cab of Fritz's truck, practically all her history class came along singing "Golden Slumbers."

Rinehart also rode in the cab. Then he climbed out to carry Zan's suitcase full of shoes to slamdunk on the finish line. He asked the other kids to pipe down, please, so he could give Zan his pep talk. They didn't so he didn't.

"Like, write Zan a letter."

"Good luck on your driver's test," Zan called to DumDum.

"Ditto you tomorrow in L.A.," Fritz yelled over the crowd.

## 10

Of course, Zan wasn't flying to Los Angeles.

Not yet.

On her plane to Olympia, Washington, Zan ran the women's marathon trials by tracing her index finger over the solid line of the course map. Rinehart had folded it among pages of tactics in his Log. He'd given Zan the suggestion that she psych herself by touching the course's turns over and over. There were lots of them.

The streets and roads of Olympia felt smooth under Zan's finger. She knew they were well-kept asphalt, no potholes or cracks.

# THE COURSE

BUDD INLET

PRIEST POINT PARK

GULF HARBOR RD. NE

26TH AVE. NE

SLEATER KINNER RD.

BIGELOW LAKE

8TH AVE. NE

EAST BAY DR.

ST. MARTIN'S COLLEGE

5TH AVE.

CAPITOL LAKE

FINISH

WASHINGTON STATE CAPITOL

COLLEGE ST. SE

START

CHAMBERS LAKE

OLYMPIA BREWERY

3RD AVE.

NORTH ST.

BARNES LAKE

SMITH LAKE

TROSPER LAKE

YELM HWY SE

LITTLEROCK RD. SW

CAPITOL BLVD.

HEWITT LAKE

W. ISRAEL

MUNN LAKE

Rinehart had found out about the course by mail from the Women's Marathon Trials Association and also that the course would be bordered with fir trees and lakes in rural neighborhoods. He'd pleaded with Zan not to be distracted by her perfect views of the Olympic Mountain range to the northwest or by the Cascades to the east.

"Don't waste your lungs on scenery raving 'Ooh' and 'Ah.' Wear your mental blinders," Rinehart had coached her.

"Yes, sir. My Zanblinders," she'd promised.

Zan licked her index finger and ran it around Budd Inlet, hoping there'd be a marine breeze for the final miles tomorrow. She dug fingernails into the finish line.

"Third." She wrote that with her nail in the middle of Capitol Lake. She borrowed a pencil from the stewardess to draw gray whiskers on a photo of Julie Brown. Zan had snitched the photo from her history-class bulletin board. "How many world-class athletes are running against you in the trials?" she asked Julie's bearded face, and answered, "One more than you've heard of before —Zan Hagen."

By the time her plane landed, Zan had used the pencil to touch up her entire collection of famous American runners. American record holder Joan Benoit wore a beard to her shorts. Zan entered the airport expecting to see her opponents looking like Father Time.

The trials committeeman who met Zan's plane was clean-shaven. He drove her to a downtown hotel and said he'd be back to accompany a group of runners over the racecourse. Would Zan care to go along on the bus?

Yes and no. Zan had done the trials course hundreds of times in Rinehart's Log but she knew from Rinehart the advantage of checking it out in person for unexpected hazards. Yes, she'd go. No, no, she wouldn't. According to Rinehart she must have nothing to do with her competition. She already held an edge by being unknown. If other runners noticed her super-well-trained body, they'd guess she was fast fast. They'd key on her in the race.

Then today she'd wear her baggiest sweat suit.

But if other runners heard her asking detailed questions on the bus they'd discover how serious she was about making the United States team.

She'd keep her mouth shut.

Then they'd guess by how hard she stared out the bus window. Hmm. But at that same time she'd be drawing conclusions about them. Whew! Zan needed her coach for a decision.

Zan went along on the bus tour even though Rinehart might have had a fit to see her sitting among her enemies. She wore a raincoat. She buried her mouth in a bus seat when she was seized with an impulse to talk about tomorrow's race. Listening, she heard:

"Tremendous racing weather. Fifty-four degrees."

"Outstanding air quality."

"Divinely flat course."

"A course to die over."

One runner after another said, "Excellent," about the view of Mt. Rainier.

Preppies surrounded her, Zan was thinking. Preppy words and preppy clothes. They had hairless faces so they must not be training on steroids. They sat whispering with their coaches, husbands, or boyfriends, holding hands, some of them. Zan shot them glances when she stood up for a better view out the bus's front window. Ahead on Ruddell Road ran the tightest pack of women Zan had ever seen.

"It's Joanie."

"Who?"

"Where?"

"The one in the Boston Marathon T-shirt."

Zan got a first fast peak at the American record holder —probably world record holder—for the women's marathon. Joan Benoit wasn't wearing any sort of beard or mustache, as nearly as could be judged from the passing bus. "We're not going as fast as I'll blow past Benoit tomorrow," Zan mumbled to her bus-seat partner.

"How fast you planning to run?"

"As fast as I can." Zan gave out no other information, said nothing but "Thanks" to the trials committeeman for her 26-mile, 385-yard trip around Olympia.

And at the pre-race meal that same evening, Zan sat apart from the crowd. She tried to eat her spaghetti noiselessly. Slurping would get attention. So would gazing around at the center table, which Zan badly wanted to do in order to catch another look at Joan Benoit, nearly engulfed by people waiting for her autograph, for training secrets and other attentions. Zan tried to figure who over there in the crowd would be a challenge tomorrow. Zan ate and hoped that asking for a second helping might go unnoticed if she slipped into line—

Uh-oh. Into the spaghetti line behind Julie Brown.

"Hi, Jules." "Hi, Brownie." "Hi, Dr. Brown." "Hi, J.B." Everyone in the hotel banquet room greeted Julie. Even the boyfriends seemed to be friends with this soft-spoken woman in a blue warm-up suit. Zan backed away from the merrymakers and decided to go hungry rather than be drawn into conversation with the main person she'd trounce tomorrow, haha.

Brown's eyes never cracked a smile. She looked intense. Worse, she looked swift. Standing absolutely still she looked swifter than anyone table-hopping in the banquet room. Brown's hair sprang from her head as if she were running in the wind: her brown every-strand-in-place hair. If Ruby Jean Twilly had come to Olympia with Zan, she'd be shrieking for a hairdo exactly like Brown's.

Brown also had freckles. Maybe freckles were covering up the evidence of steroids. Hmm.

"Hi, Julie. What bad news for the U.S. did you bring home from your racing wars abroad?" asked a photographer eating at the nearby press table.

Julie Brown smiled, except with her eyes. A man waiting in line next to her answered, "You've already heard about China's young girl, who's run a dozen mediocre three-hour marathons and the one she ran clocked at 2:20, according to *Tiyo Bao*? As long as the People's Republic holds her stopwatch we can't be certain of the times."

"She's their secret weapon," another man called from the press table. "Their China Nuke."

Julie laughed, except with her eyes. She said, "Her world record's awesome," in the quietest voice Zan had ever heard. "She's a nice person," Julie added.

"Twelve years younger than Julie is, an untested product of China's junior program. We met her once at a state dinner, not on the track. Please, let Julie eat her carbos." Brown's coach steered his athlete to a remote table.

Nighty-night, Julie, Zan thought while riding the hotel elevator to her room. Once there she swallowed a capsule that Rinehart had filled for her in his lab and swore would put her to sleep but Zan knew was pure brown sugar. She undressed, went to bed, didn't sleep, sat up to watch a woman named Switzer on TV who talked about the trials tomorrow. Zan's name wasn't mentioned by Switzer as a "hot tip for top honors."

"That's all you know," Zan told the tube before chewing another pill and her fingernails, lying down, sitting up to dial Rinehart's phone number without the area code, hearing a buzz, hanging up, lying down, reviewing her race plan, sleeping, waking up to run, at 9:15 Pacific time, in the Women's Olympic Marathon Trials in Olympia, Washington, U.S.A.

Zan followed her pre-race ritual written in Rinehart's
Log:

1. Phone room service for hot tea and iced juice.
   Drink them slowly while stretching for 15 minutes.
2. Take a long, lukewarm shower. Take two aspirins.
3. Smear Vaseline under bra straps in case they rub.
   Make sure straps are not loose, not tight.
4. Suit up in gray shorts and shirt. Use nail scissors
   to trim extra paper from around race number. Pin
   trimmed number on shirt.
5. Use Johnson's Baby Powder on feet. Put on socks.
   Adjust them in shoes. Socks must not rub. Tighten
   shoelaces (not too tight). Tie them in triple knots.

Zan took a break to put a √ beside the first five numbers. She wondered if, in St. Martin's College nearby,
where the fastest qualifiers were staying in the dorm,
Brown and Benoit were getting ready this same way.
Maybe instead of fussing around they had huge free
breakfasts on silver trays served to them, who knows?

Zan understood from Rinehart's experiments on her
that eating breakfast this morning would give her a side
stitch at mile 10. Further, she knew from his research
that her feet blistered without socks and that every extra
teensy ounce carried for twenty-six miles would tire her
sooner. Zan snatched her scissors again to cut the label
out of her shorts—uh-oh. She had them on backward.
Blister City in three miles from rubbing.

Changing her shorts around, Zan wondered if other

runners understood that pink and mauve were bad-luck colors. Lucky for Zan that Ruby Jean had explained astrologically correct colors for a Gemini and that E.J. had sent along Johnson's Baby Powder. Not quite "Johnston" like E.J.'s name but close enough.

"What're the other runners doing right now?" Zan asked the bathroom mirror. She squeezed toothpaste on her brush but said, "Don't do it." Fritz Slappy had given Zan his favorite psych-up: scuzzy teeth. The feeling of unbrushed teeth all race would make her tough, he'd swore.

Zan popped a pill instead of brushing. She sucked the brown sugar. She still had time to write Rinehart a postcard. She wrote him that she'd won the trials. She packed the postcard in her suitcase because she'd be arriving home in Arlington ahead of any mail. She'd hand Rinehart the card late tonight at National Airport.

6. Put on sweat suit. Zip zippers.
7. Report to starting line of race. Jog there slowly for a warm-up.

On her way, Zan waved to ABC Sports outside the hotel. She passed some kids handing out Dole pineapples. Dole was sponsoring this race she knew from T-shirts and banners. She passed Mary Shea. Zan flew past thousands who'd come to see the race start and end here.

"How's my chance today?" "Mine?" "Mine?" asked runners stretching in a circle around Benoit.

"Fine—glorious—terrific—" said the TV Switzer

from a platform above the starting line. She talked into a microphone pinned to the collar of her dress.

Zan remembered from Rinehart's reading that a K. Switzer had been the first woman ever to register for and then run in the Boston Marathon. Years and years ago, before Zanbaby took her first step. What fun it would be to leap up beside Switzer now and say, "Hi, Mom!"

Monk, Aileen, Lurleen, and the others would be absorbed in this Saturday-morning TV program at Dum-Dum's house. He was taping the race on his Betamax. He'd replay it at midnight tonight with pretzels, Nachos, Moon Pies, Chipwiches, and the other junk food Zan had missed badly during training.

"Sweats off, ladies" came a man's voice over the loudspeaker.

Zan disobeyed. She continued to follow Rinehart's pre-race schedule.

8. Find a tree. Stretch hamstrings and quadriceps using the tree trunk to work against.

Many other women were still jogging, sprinting, or waiting in line for bathrooms until they heard, "To your marks, ladies." Zan noticed that only Joan Benoit already stood in the front row of the starting line. She chatted with the dozens in row 2.

9. Unzipper sweat suit. Remove without wiping away Vaseline. Leave suit with official. Find start-

ing place at the back of the herd alongside other 2:50 qualifiers.

By hopping on her tiptoes, Zan could see over the rows and rows of runners in front of her. Three press trucks were about to roll with the lead car topped with a trunk-sized digital clock set at 0:00:00. Rinehart had explained to Zan that if she kept the clock in sight and stayed alert for the mile markers, she'd know her pace the entire twenty-six miles.

Watching the clock meant running with the leaders.

## 10. Go.

The clean air of Olympia, Washington, smelled like cap-pistol smoke. Zan hadn't been listening for the starting gun. She'd been concentrating on Rinehart's instructions to leave the starting line smoothly in the flow of bodies surrounding her; go gently to save herself from accidentally losing a shoe in the crowd of three hundred. Most of the runners started in front of Zan and stayed there until the crowd thinned into lines, the lines into clumps, the clumps into twos and threes. Then Zan patiently worked her way to a lead pair of runners who seemed to be blazing the trail.

Nothing to it. In less than three miles of the trial marathon, Zan was running right up there behind front-runners Joan Benoit and Julie Brown. Without the entourage around Benoit, Zan could see and admire her jaunty footplants—whew—her whole cocky running style. Good to think about that. And about Brown's movements as soft as her voice. Zan kept her mind full of these leaders and the mile markers and the pain.

Pain was on its way. It couldn't be avoided at this pace. Zan ran within striking distance of two of the world's fastest women. Rinehart sure had predicted their race plan. They followed the clock. Everyone else in this Olympic trial followed Zan's third place.

# 11

"The 20-mile mark is where a marathon really begins," Zan heard Rinehart's voice telling her as she passed a green sign painted 20. She wouldn't have needed the marker. Zan knew how far she'd run because she was hitting the wall.

Call it a wall; call it any other word; it meant pain. And not just the nagging little chest aches and leg spasms of the first twenty miles, either. Now Zan's toes and fingers tingled and stung. She felt queasy, lightheaded, close to fainting. She moved west on Gull Harbor Road thinking the only good thing about the wall was that both front-runners had also hit it. Their muscles, like hers, were running out of fuel. Their pain would increase, ha ha, until their last stride.

So would hers.

Zan had a magic way to deal with the pain. Did Joan Benoit? Did Julie Brown?

How could they have without Rinehart for their coach? He'd taught Zan that the best way to handle pain in a race was to think about it and about nothing else. "Think about your difficult breathing," he'd patiently taught her on his treadmill. "Don't try to distract yourself from your heavy thighs. Don't tell yourself jokes. Don't let your mind wander from what your body's feeling. Stay in touch with pain so you can monitor how much energy you have left."

They're dead up ahead, Zan decided from how her own body felt. "Dead," she told spectators lining the street two deep at mile 22. "They're faking it."

Julie Brown ran with the same sense of grace she had from the start. Joan Benoit still appeared to be running with ease, with naturalness. They led Zan now by only ten yards. Zan could catch them. She could pass them and take over first place if Rinehart would let her.

Ah, this reviving marine breeze off Puget Sound!

What would Rinehart say if I ran up between Joan and Julie? Zan was asking herself.

He'd say, "Don't pass them. Follow my strategy to the finish," and strike his glasses against his Log. E.J. would agree with, "Great idea." But Fritz would be hollering. "Croak the jerks," and DumDum would be pressing his

gas-pedal foot against his Betamax, and Lurleen would
be squealing:

> Gimme a *first*,
> Gimme a first place at the Olympics.

Not second.

Not third.

Zan was moving closer to the front-runners. She
couldn't help it.

They were coming back to her.

Now what? What to do at mile 24? What would
Rinehart order her to do? Zan tried to remember his
Log. She tried to feel how much power was left in her
calves, which seemed to give off sparks of fatigue. The
digital clock on the pace car read 2:11:00 with two miles
left in the race. Zan had a shot at the world record, she
figured out by subtracting 2:11:00 from 2:22:16—
Benoit's record, not the secret-weapon Chinese one. But
to go for the record she'd have to take over the lead.
She'd need to bolt—no, not to bolt—she all of a sudden
had an unobstructed view of the clock because Benoit
had fallen behind her and Brown ran even with Zan's
left wrist. Zan couldn't help noticing Brown's every hair
in place after twenty-five miles of striding. Brown didn't
have whiskers, either, Zan could see under the zigzags
of sweat on her freckles.

Stride for stride, they ran half a mile.

Then Brown did something Zan would never have done: she looked back over her shoulder.

"Kick—or—we're—going—to—be—passed."

Zan heard that but didn't believe Julie's gasps. "A psych-out," Zan mumbled. Why should a racer warn a competitor? In this race of all races, why should Brown help Zan? It could only be a trick.

Zan listened for someone behind her. She heard nothing but Julie's butterfly footplants. And the crowd.

Zan thought to herself she should turn around and look.

Only runners afraid to lose look back.

I am first, Zan insisted with her feet. She stayed on her same pace. Rinehart had commanded her to. She could hear him from Arlington. She didn't need to think about anything but her own ten-ton shoes, which must be picked up and put down for another half mile.

She didn't need to think about Brown, who was kicking past her.

Help!

Or think about Benoit springing past.

I'm third after all, Zan admitted to herself. She could almost hear Ruby Jean Twilly saying, "Poor you." Zan did hear people screaming. They spilled from the sidewalks onto the course, leaving only a narrow passageway for Zan to run the remaining four hundred yards of her race.

They were screaming encouragement for a runner trying to edge Zan for third.

Zan felt an elbow brushing her arm. She felt a stinging elbow in her ribs. She felt a body as wet as her own. It shoved and slithered between her and the spectators. The crowd shoved Zan, closing around her.

Zan had no room on either side to pass the runner in third place.

What to do now?

It's too late to think, Zan thought.

Zan followed the third-place finisher across the line and into the chute.

## 12

While Zan waited by her suitcase in National Airport, she revised the one post-card she'd written on her disastrous trip West: "Dear Rinehart. I won. Guess who."

She crossed out "won" and put "lost." She didn't sign it with a tear. Zan was pretending she didn't care. She couldn't cry in front of Fritz's whole truckful of her friends when they arrived to meet her tonight. "I don't care . . . caresies," she rehearsed saying. She pulled two pairs of running shoes from her suitcase and spiked them against an airport bench she'd taken over to wait on.

One hour later Zan was still there. She'd had plenty of

time to say, "Caresies," in her raincoat, which she was
using for a waterproof pillow. She'd changed Rinehart's
postcard from "Guess who" to "Fourth Hagen." When
he eventually found her, Zan was retrieving her Nikes
and giving them away to little kids who shouldn't be
staying up this late at night.

"Have you seen a guy in a checkered jacket and earmuffs?" Zan was asking around everywhere.

Rinehart himself hurried toward her, answering, "It's
May 12. I haven't worn earmuffs since winter." He
didn't say anything about her fourth place. He picked
up Zan's suitcase and led her to the metro. He paid for
them both. During their ride he didn't explain why Fritz
and the others hadn't come to meet her. He mentioned
only that DumDum had failed his driver's test.

"Then he won't be competing in the Drivers' Olympics," said Zan.

She caught the school bus next day. She said, "What
do I care?" to the driver. She'd never seen him before.
She said, "Tough on me," in homeroom. F. Parnell
Manfred got Zan's race time and her finishing position
correct for a change in his morning announcements.

"No matter our dear Suzanne's failure, I, personally,
am attending the summer Olympics in Los Angeles
inasmuch as I am a frugal man. I give you my word not
to squander the tickets that you, my inspired student-
athletes of Robert E. Lee, presented to me as a token—"

Zan wasn't even thinking, Fruitcake.

She took her mind off her failure by painstakingly

gluing the heads, arms, legs, and feet onto the photos of her running opponents. She'd torn them apart on the metro last night. It seemed likely that Mrs. Tunis would ask for them back. Zan also glued together a photo of herself she'd torn up from this morning's *Herald*.

"Great stride," E.J. said of Zan's picture.

"Not all that great." Zan used her pencil to poke Brown's eyes from her photo. She stuck them into her own eyesockets. "Check me out with these serious Brown eyes."

"She was great on television yesterday. We watched the race at Walter's."

"Did it show where Brown looked over her shoulder? Where she saw the second pack coming at us? Where she warned me that Benoit and another girl were kicking?" Zan couldn't say the name of the third-place winner.

"The end happened so fast. People were everywhere on the route. They wandered into the camera's way, I imagine."

Zan didn't say, "Plus in my way." She wasn't making excuses for her loss. When you place fourth in a foot-race, there's only one reason: you didn't run as fast as the first three.

No excuses.

Yet. On her way to first period, Zan tried to fake reasons for not making the United States team. She had to tell the kids something. Hmm. Water stations? Officials?

Weather? These had been perfect. She hadn't over-trained or undertrained.

She could grumble about crowd control. Or her young age, okay. One of the youngest in the trials.

Her ex-teammate from the Lee Generals Randy Boyle was not much older than Zan and already he was a New York Yankee. Song Mai was Zan's age and already on China's track team, Zan reminded herself by looking at the world map in history. She tacked Brown and Benoit back beside their light bulbs.

"Wait'll next year," DumDum was predicting.

E.J. explained to him, "Olympics are every four years. Zan can't try again until—"

"Nope, not Olympics. We're talking driver's license here. Me, I'll do the test over again in August."

"Too true," said Mrs. Tunis. She opened her lecture by reviewing for the final exam. Olympics weren't mentioned, except in a whisper by Ruby Jean Twilly. "Us majorettes canceled our float dresses 'cause you bombed, Zan. Sorry."

"I'm probably sorrier," Zan replied. Lurleen Dewey passed her a note that Zan wrinkled up and ate instead of reading. So I lost, she thought. Caresies. Zan tried to make her face unreadable like Brown's and Mrs. Tunis's.

When the bell rang, Fritz boogalooed past Zan's desk, heading for the bulletin board. He pulled the plug on Europe. "You lose," he said to Zan.

He pulled the plug on Asia. "Ditto all these foreigners. They stuck it to you, Zan babe."

"I didn't even run against them."

"That's the point. You won't get to."

"Wait'll four years from now." Zan hoped her voice sounded chipper.

Mrs. Tunis helped her. "Yesterday Ms. Hagen defeated every woman but a few in a field of several hundred. Furthermore, she defeated every other American woman citizen who did not go to the state of Washington to race. Over one hundred million women. These individuals each have two legs, lungs, a heart, and a mind. They might well have trained to race. But they chose not to. Thus they did not qualify to race against Ms. Hagen yesterday at the trials."

She's finally got it straight about trials, Zan thought on her way to Spanish. She's separated them from the Olympics in the nick of time because trials are over and I'm over, caresies.

In Spanish class Zan greeted Monk with "Numero Fouro."

"Adios Goldo Medalo." He gave Zan a hug anyway and promised to listen to her reasons at lunchtime—about Julie Brown, etc.

E.J. and Monk had saved their usual private table in the cafeteria but Zan couldn't face them again, or Rinehart either, with his briefcase of drawings of who-might-have-been-doing-what in the final mile. Zan had been over and over the drawings last night on the metro until she swore to Rinehart she'd never run a marathon again. Not Boston. Not Seoul, Korea, in the next summer

Olympics *only* four years away. Not even Los Angeles this August 5 if the U.S. coach came to her in person and pled that America needed her to wipe out Communist marathoners single-handed. China, whoever, Zan wouldn't care. She'd just refuse.

In that mood Zan took her lunch out to Lee High track. She'd eat alone.

The school year was coming to an end. Kids lolled around in the top bleachers reviewing for exams, sunning themselves, pointing to the starting line and talking behind their books. Zan raised a fist over her head. "Dump on me all you want," she shouted. She'd have thrown her milk carton if Mrs. Tunis hadn't stepped into lane 1 ahead of her.

"How could I resist timing your laps on such an aromatic morning?"

"I'm not sprinting ever again. Why should I? I happen to be out of Olympic contention." Zan eyed her teacher for a reaction.

"I saw the telecast yesterday."

"So I didn't take drugs like the others. So?" Zan gave this desperate excuse she knew couldn't be disputed, not by some history teacher, anyway. Not without urine tests.

"I might have laid your fourth-place appearance at other doors."

Zan looked baffled. She tried again with, "Steroids."

"Rather than fault the winners, you might well shoulder the blame yourself."

"Me?"

"I dare say."

Zan started walking as fast as she knew how. "I don't care what you dare say. I've quit racing forever, and P.S., I do blame myself. I lost. Me, Zanbomber. Julie Brown didn't even have stubble to beat me with."

Mrs. Tunis unfastened a pocketbook she always carried over her arm when not in the classroom. She pulled out a handful of 3 x 5 cards. "My research notes." She spoke pleasantly. "Teachers give assignments to themselves." She read:

John A. Kelley   18th in the Berlin Olympics in 2:49

John A. Kelley   21st in the London Olympics in 2:51

"Observe that this man Kelley, an American, ran far back in the field at his first Olympics. Even so, he continued to train for another Olympics twelve years later."

Zan couldn't have cared less. "Oh, yeah, sure. What happened to him in all the Olympics in between Berlin and London? Bet he was boohooing about messing up."

"There were no Olympic Games from 1936 to 1948. World War II intervened. Athletics took second place to killing. Now, see here about Mr. Kenneth Moore. He writes for *Sports Illustrated*, I discover.

Kenny Moore   14th in Mexico City in 2:29

Kenny Moore   4th in Munich in 2:15

"Neither did Mr. Moore give up running after his marathon in Mexico. He strove to improve his showing. What's more, he did."

"Fourth stinks."

"It's not his place I'm bringing to your attention so much as Mr. Moore himself, his continuing determination in defeat. Nor was Mr. Moore's teammate, Frank Shorter, a quitter in his triumph.

Frank Shorter   1st in Munich in 2:12
Frank Shorter   2nd in Montreal in 2:10

"As a follower of Mr. Shorter, you certainly recall that he "lost" the marathon at his second Olympics? If his silver medal in Montreal can be considered losing."

Losses?

Wins?

Wars?

Marathons?

Zan couldn't tell them apart at this moment. All she knew was, she was heartbroken. Dying, in fact. She sank down on the track and wept.

Her world-history teacher did not sink alongside her. No indeed. Mrs. Tunis deposited her purse on the curb and set out on a rickety run around Lee track. Her form was impossible. Her skirt kept her knees from lifting. She hardly moved her arms. They remained at her sides, her wrists locked in the same position as she might use dunking crumpets in tea. Cinders crunched heavily under her thick-soled Top-Siders.

"Go, Teach, go" drifted from the bleachers.

Into the far straight Mrs. Tunis continued her ungainly movements, slower and slower. Distance at last caught up with her. She stopped to take off a sweater, to arrange it over one arm like a waiter's towel. As she began running again, the top bleachers rippled with laughter.

Zan sat up to see who could be laughing at Zanbomber. They'd pay. Zan might be full of sorrow, but nobody was going to rub it in about her dismal TV performance yesterday. Nobody could get away with pointing at her—hey, not at her. That's Mrs. Tunis going lickety-split they're laughing at, Zan noticed. She wasn't embarrassed for her teacher. Any effort at running impressed Zan, who remembered how a billion footsteps on Lee track felt. Each step took willpower. A person's mind had to decide to pick up the right foot, put down the left, no matter how strained lungs were. "Atta girl," Zan shouted to Mrs. Tunis in the home straightaway.

She looked dreadfully tired.

But she didn't quit. She handed Zan the sweater. "It begins to dawn on me what running demands of one's body."

"Point your toes," Zan answered. "Your feet flop sideways. They're throwing your body off balance. You're losing tenths of seconds each step."

"Like this?"

"Just walk," Zan called. "Practice pointing your feet straight ahead." She walked around the near curve with her teacher.

"I am one of those who rarely ran as a child. My generation of little girls was, shall I say, unhurried."

"Use your arms."

"May I ask how?"

"Like this." Zan loped off ahead. "Your arms lead you. Check this." She exaggerated her moves for ten yards, trotting back to Mrs. Tunis with, "Look at how I'm moving. Think about it."

They moved together and thought, both of them, for a lap. Their rhythm of uninterrupted strides, their level conversation about their form set the stage for Mrs. Tunis to observe, "The concluding moment of your marathon yesterday—it remains unilluminated to me as a viewer."

"Me too."

"Would it be hurtful to confide why you didn't make the U.S. team?"

"I faded."

"Ms. Brown couldn't explain your concluding tactics in her interview after the race. And you were 'unavailable for comment,' according to Ms. Switzer."

"I beat it out of the chute. Plus out of our hotel before the awards ceremony. I flew right home."

Mrs. Tunis jogged to a place slightly ahead of Zan. "Let us pretend I am Ms. Brown and you are hurrying up beside her as you did yesterday."

"She was coming back to me."

"The commentator did mention that she was slowing in her twenty-third mile. And so you ran next to each other as we are doing. When she ran past you, what made you decide not to stay near her?"

"Rinehart. His strategy. His voice in my ear. He coached me to stay behind the two leaders. He knew Brown and Benoit would front-run. They'd pace me. I could tell their time from the pace clock. We were right on the time Rinehart predicted would bring them in one-two and me in third. If I'd kicked like a superstar to beat them, I'd be world-famous. But then Russia and them would take me out too fast and grind me down early at the Olympics. Rinehart said so."

Zan wasn't sure all this had been asked for, but she continued. "Benoit dropped off. I didn't know how far. I don't look back. Brown stayed with me, for my company, I guess. It's hard to front-run a whole marathon. It's lonely. She let me pull her along those last miles. She looked over her shoulder and saw Benoit. Plus she must have seen the whole second pack charging us. Brown warned me."

"Warned? How so?"

"She talked, if you call it talking. Why waste air? It's dumb. It took forever for her to say, 'They're passing us,' something like that. I didn't believe her. Any runner that helps any other one's a loser."

"Ms. Brown, however, did not lose."

"Listen, I thought she was trying to psych me out."

"And was she, in retrospect?"

"I guess not. She passed me. Benoit did, too, right after

that, and some other girl. By the time I got my as—
myself in gear, they'd left me in their dust, the whole
three. I didn't have a higher gear to catch them with, and
anyway, there wasn't room. You saw."

Mrs. Tunis stopped in her tracks. "This account you
give is well worth thinking over. The chain of events.
Your inability to decide for yourself during a race. Your
response to another runner's help. Your unwillingness to
look back."

"That stuff stinks. What about high gear? I didn't
have it."

Mrs. Tunis made no remark.

"Anyway, I won't need kicking gears ever again. I'm
aiming to be an ordinary foot soldier in history. A
slouchy walker like us. Who cares?"

If Mrs. Tunis cared she didn't say it in so many words.
She asked for a demonstration of how a runner might
glance behind in a race and still be able to propel herself
forward. She asked Zan if her decision not to turn around
to see other runners might be tinged with arrogance. She
wanted Zan to repeat typical considerate comments she'd
heard in athletic contests and typical nasty remarks. She
was curious to know if Mr. Rinehart's strategies ever included occasions when Zan had to think for herself.

Zan lapped the track and tried to answer, until a bell
rang in the distance. Mrs. Tunis was due in her second-
floor room. Zan could very well abandon her schooling
for athletic training, but Mrs. Tunis must meet her afternoon classes.

"I gave my racing shoes away," Zan said about strategy. They walked toward the building. Entering Lee High, Mrs. Tunis referred one more time to her research cards:

> Abebe Bikila    1st in Rome in 2:15:16
> Abebe Bikila    1st in Tokyo in 2:12:11

"Mr. Bikila ran barefooted," she added from memory. Zan said, "Gimme a break."

# 13

On May 17 Zan received a postcard from Julie Brown. One side had a picture of St. Martin's College in Olympia. The other side, printed in blue pencil, contained this message:

Dear Suzanne,
   The trials director gave me your address. I hope this gets to you in Virginia. I hunted around the press tent to tell you how well you raced against us old veterans. At your age I only raced the ½ mile and mile. Well, maybe we'll see each other in Bos-

ton next Patriots' Day for the marathon. I hope. Happy running.

> Love,
> Julie B.

"Awesome card," Zan told Rinehart. She was speaking to him again.

He was speaking to her again. "If I coached Julie Brown I'd still be going to L.A. Except I can't afford a ticket anymore."

Next day, May 18, a letter arrived from someone Zan had never heard of: "Greetings from Uncle Sam," it began. Zan thought, I don't have any uncles named Sam. It's the wrong address. Yet she kept reading, because she hardly ever found a letter in her room when she came home from school.

"As you know, I am the Women's Olympic Long and Middle Distance Teams' coach and in that capacity I am alerting you to the possibility of your running for the United States of America in Los Angeles."

"Sounds like Rinehart," Zan grumbled to the letter she'd spread on the foot of her bed. "Some trick." She skipped to the end sentence.

"You will hear from me or directly from Brooks Johnson, head coach of our Women's Olympic Track and Field Team, if and when the team should need you. Sincerely, Doris B. Heritage."

"Rinehart for sure." Zan jumped into her old basketball Keds and ran to Rinehart's house to deliver his letter back. Down in his laboratory she caught him studying a Betamax videotape he'd bought from DumDum. "I cashed in my L.A. plane ticket, chipped in my hotel and taxi money to lay hands on this scientific equipment," said Rinehart, tapping his ruler against the screen of a brand-new TV.

Zan thrust her letter at him. "Did you forge me this?"

With one glance Rinehart took in the letter's main paragraph. "Says you're to remain in competitive shape . . . consult with your coach . . . says that if something happens to any of the three women who finished with better times than you in the trials . . . you're an alternate . . . ALTERNATE ON THE UNITED STATES OLYMPIC TEAM." Rinehart let out a "Whuppee."

"What's that? An alternate?"

"Says you'll be running for the U.S. if one of the other three can't."

"You're kidding me."

Rinehart socked himself in the head. "And I sold back my plane ticket."


School let out for summer vacation the morning of June 5. That evening the Hagens' phone rang from California.

" 'Lo."

"Miss Suzanne Hagen, please."

"This is me."

"Hold the line for Brooks Johnson from Stanford University. Among other things, he'd like to know what size running shoe you wear."

"Size 8." Zan tried to think if Rinehart could be faking a long-distance call to keep her in training for research on his experimental Kick and Shove. She listened for the crackling of long-distance wires.

"This is Brooks Johnson in Palo Alto. How are you?" The man's voice was friendly.

"Okay."

"We're now anticipating a slot on our marathon team owing to a bothersome hamstring. Case in point, our number-three runner. My own feeling is that she'll not be ready to race as early as this coming August 5."

Zan asked, "Are you really in California?"

In the time between Coach Johnson's "Yes" and Zan's "Oh" she heard the crackling wires, three thousand miles of them. He continued with, "There have been numerous instances of last-minute substitutions on the U.S. Olympic teams. You may be asked to play a strategic role. As alternate, you're next in line."

"I'm training a lot."

"Paying your dues, eh? Essentially, what are your workouts?"

Zan described the schedule she'd been on since she ended her retirement the noon after she began it. She glossed over her routine distance and speed drills. "Too dull to tell a person in swell California," she explained.

She talked up her "own personal coach, Arthur Rinehart of Robert E. Lee High. She explained how Rinehart was using a videotape of her trial marathon to prove his point about her feeble kick. "Rinehart's coaching me to use my hands to kick with."

"Original."

Zan heard the wires again. Whew—her first phone call ever from California!

"We believe your coaching has contributed immeasurably to the runner you are, a 2:26 marathoner. Far be it from me or my staff to interfere. Yet there's always room for improvement."

"Hmm."

"Call me collect if you need our help. Oh, and keep me informed of your physical condition. I'll get back to you about your team status. Goodbye."

" 'Bye."

Zan said " 'lo" to Rinehart in practically the same breath. She'd run to his house faster than yesterday when, out of habit, she'd timed herself with her wrist stopwatch. Today she sat on a weight bench to watch the last mile of his Betamax trials—watch for the billionth time. When Zan mentioned what Brooks Johnson had said about the third-place girl, Rinehart wasn't surprised.

He pointed his scalpel at the TV screen. "Diagnose her hamstring yourself. See, as she crosses the line. No, don't be disgusted with your finish. You're behind but you're healthy. She's in pain. Her fingers automatically reach back and grab her hamstring." Rinehart zoomed in on Number Three's right leg.

On a small screen in her coach's basement, Zan saw the reason she had to train for another two months. "Should I hope her hamstring gets worse so I make the team?" Zan asked herself as much as Rinehart.

"I'll hope for us both. Don't waste calories thinking about the future. Your energy must go into workouts." Rinehart punched a button to put Number Three in freeze frame. He said, "I hope I hope I hope."


A UPS truck pulled up in front of the Hagens' house on June 15. Zan happened to be in the driveway stretching before her morning run to summer-school Spanish. She had time to open a package addressed to her. Out tumbled eight running shoes, tied together in pairs. Each pair was slightly different in weight, Zan discovered from hefting them. They were each blue with three white stripes. They all smelled the same. A Xeroxed note on Adidas stationery read:

Dear Miss Hagen:
Your name has been referred to us by Brooks Johnson. We supply, free of charge, athletic shoes for the United States Olympic teams. The enclosed have been designed specifically for the Los Angeles marathon course, which, except for its beginning and ending on synthetic track surfaces, is asphalt over the entire length of its 26 miles, 385 yards.

"Tell me about its length," Zan said with an exhausted "whew."

> In making your selection of a competition shoe, take into consideration the thickness/depth of heel counter you regularly demand as a cushion for heel strike. Balance the comfort of a slightly heavier shoe against the extra ounces thus carried the marathon distance. Allow a normal break-in period of fifty miles for your shoes before the most important marathon this century.
>
> Sincerely,

"Let Rinehart choose my shoes," said Zan to the UPS man waiting for her to sign his delivery slip. "I'll give away the other pairs to E.J. and Monk when they come home from summer vacation."

Zan put on the shoes with the thinnest soles for her run to Spanish class, but she didn't make it there. F. Parnell Manfred waylaid her near his office. "A singular favor, Suzanne?" he asked. He dangled a large white envelope decorated with a gold lightning bolt. "This express-mailer arrived for your wonderful friend Rinehart. Shall we have a peak inside?" He flashed Zan the address label typed COACH ARTHUR RINEHART. Manfred whispered, "I pray there's nothing too seriously the matter."

It flitted through Zan's mind that she might hint to her principal about being an alternate on the Olympic team.

But no, he'd go and brag her up around Arlington County the way he did before her Durham fiasco. And then if Zan didn't race—and she probably wouldn't—she'd look nuttier than Manfred.

Zan's own best friends didn't know she might race. E.J. was up in Vermont at basketball camp. Monk didn't correspond with Zan from his church leadership conference in somewhere named Santa Cruz. Lurleen and Ruby Jean spent every summer at Virginia Beach. They'd gone without saying "See ya." Fritz Slappy had joined the U.S. Navy and left before he even took his final exams. None of them suspected Zan's last hope to race in L.A., nor did DumDum, and he went to summer-school history class right across the hall from Zan's Spanish.

Just as well no one knew about L.A., because Zan probably wouldn't be racing. She wasn't getting anyone's hopes up, especially her own. Anyway, hoping wastes energy! That was Rinehart's law.

All the same, Zan lunged at Mr. Manfred for the envelope. "I'll deliver it," she said, and ran for Rinehart's lab.


Mailmen don't make their rounds on the Fourth of July so Zan didn't moon away that afternoon waiting at the Hagens' mailbox. Rinehart didn't stand guard over his, either. They used Zan's vacation day from Spanish to study their epic Betamax tape. Rinehart had labeled it *Zan's Mis-Trial*.

Studied and listened for Rinehart's phone to ring.

"You sure it's today they'll be calling?" Zan asked more than once.

Rinehart gave her the same answer each time. "Their letter said the first week of July. That leaves the rest of today, all day tomorrow, the next day, and the next. They may call. They may write. They said, "Be in touch.""

"Maybe they'll fly in from California. Zip right on down the basement stairs to touch us both." Zan shrugged at the TV screen. "Can you figure why they didn't mention my wimpy finishing kick in their letter? Read it to me just once more."

Rinehart opened a drawer in his operating table. He extracted the envelope Zan had brought him two weeks earlier. "It's headed *Travel and Housing Committee*," he said. "Dear Mr. Rinehart: As Suzanne Hagen's coach you should be made aware of the financial arrangements intended for each member and alternate member of the United States Olympic Teams and of the check-in procedure at Olympic Village in Los Angeles, California."

The phone rang.

Zan dimmed the Betamax sound. Her own personal coach answered his phone. "Rinehart here. No. Thanks a million." He hung up and told Zan, "Walter says to turn on Channel 7. They're reporting about the Olympics on *Sportsbreak*."

The TV screen suddenly changed from Zan's hurly-burly trial finish to a commentator saying, "A rash of injuries plaguing world-class runners so far in this, our

Olympic, summer further confirms the vulnerability of athletes to intensive training."

"Heck, missed it. Maybe Number Three—" Zan mumbled.

Rinehart was already dialing DumDum. "What women were mentioned on *Sportsbreak*?" he asked. "Her? She's a sprinter. You mean her? She's a miler. Her?" Rinehart giggled. "I wouldn't call pregnancy an injury."

"Who? Number Three?" Zan used energy to keep hope from her voice.

Rinehart hung up and told Zan that the fastest South American marathoner was running even though she was pregnant.

"How'd DumDum know that?"

"Extra credit for Mrs. Tunis. Walter's taken over the bulletin board to help him get an A in history this summer. He's reading sports magazines and newspapers. I paid him off in driver-training information to staple your photo back up near the U.S. team. You're next in line. You never know. You might accidentally be running. At least you might be going to L.A. to find out if you'll run."

Rinehart's hand remained wrapped around the telephone. Maybe it would ring again.

"Please ring." Zan couldn't help getting her hopes up.

But when no word had come from California by late that evening, Zan reluctantly took her long, slow, training run, and Rinehart followed on his bike. They were forced to dodge firecrackers down Lee Highway. They had to push their way through hundreds waiting for the Fourth of July fireworks display over Francis Scott Key Bridge. "Here's the place to practice your Rinehart Kick and Shove," Rinehart coached Zan by shouting. She did what Rinehart wanted. She shoved, not once pausing to gaze skyward at the three-story-high exploding American flag. Zan kept up their speed no matter how many spectators blocked their way. Good practice for eliminating Russians, New Zealanders, Brazilians, I hope, I hope, Zan ran along thinking. She must speed back to Rinehart's lab. The phone might be ringing, I hope.

Rinehart shouted, "These patriotic fireworks—they're made in China. Gifts to our government, I read in the *Herald*. You'll watch them tonight on Betamax from the treadmill as you practice your sneaky shoves."

"I'll show China some dynamite of my own if I get the call to L.A."

Zan picked up the pace to Rinehart's phone.

Until July 24 phone calls, letters, and packages continued to break into Zan's training and to steal her attention from summer school. She'd have to repeat Spanish I in the fall, what with skipping class so often to follow instructions from Olympic chairmen and coaches.

Zan now owned a complimentary round-trip airline ticket to Los Angeles and a plane reservation for July 25.

She'd fly out early enough for the opening ceremonies. She'd taper off her training on the actual marathon course. She'd been given a room assignment in the Olympic Village. She'd been sent her U.S.A. uniform for the race and two U.S.A. warmup suits, and the credentials she'd need to prove that her name was Hagen, Suzanne, a bona fide alternate on the United States Olympic Track Team.

She was packed.

In Arlington only her parents knew about the trip, and Rinehart and DumDum, who'd alertly picked out her name from the fine print in the July *Track & Field News* he'd borrowed for "his" bulletin board. They all agreed about Zan's keeping a low profile in order not to raise Arlington's expectations for a medal. DumDum wouldn't tell Tunis, ho ho, because Zan's chances of actually competing in the Olympics seemed practically zero. And zero DumDum understood perfectly! The women who'd beaten Zan had survived their training camp in Santa Barbara, California. Number Three's hamstring might still be sore but not too sore for August 5 or Zan would have heard from Brooks Johnson.

On the afternoon of July 24, Rinehart pedaled his broken-down bike to a tree under Zan's bedroom window at home. She was upstairs practicing aloud for an oral Spanish exam she'd be taking tomorrow morning before her plane left, Olympics or no Olympics.

Rinehart shouted for her to come on down.

"*No comprendo.*"

"It's about the Olympics."

Zan's legs suddenly appeared over the windowsill.

"Don't jump. Save yourself for tomorrow. Channel 7. *Wake Up, Virginia*, that talk show. They found out from United Press wire service that you're an alternate and I'm an alternate coach. We're guest talkers. Wear your uniform the way you are now."

Zan patted the large white star on her singlet. "You call this a low profile?"

"You deserve to wear it. Don't forget you're the fourth-fastest woman marathoner in our country. You've earned a shot on TV for all those hard miles' training you've run for me."

"I might get scared of the cameras and blow it."

"You?"

"Plus I'll miss my Spanish exam."

"Channel 7 already expects you'll do your talking in Spanish. I said you're committed to 'refining your accent' for use in the Olympic's opening ceremony. They believed me. Also, I called up your Spanish teacher. He'll be listening to the TV in Manfred's office, grading you on your accent and vocabulary."

"You schemer. If only you'd schemed me into third place. Or second."

Rinehart looked too guilty for Zan to add, "Or first place." She told him she couldn't miss her plane in order to be on *Good Morning, Virginia*.

"They'll send you from the TV station in a stretch limousine after your interview."

"Maybe they'd drive me all the way to the starting line? I'd spook our enemies if I popped out of a huge black car."

Rinehart waited for Zan to come downstairs to memorize the answers he'd prepared in Spanish for their TV interview. With a sad voice he reminded her then, "You aren't starting."

# 14

ANNOUNCER: Wake up, Virginia. It's 8:30 a.m. Wednesday, July 25, and we have here today Arlington's gift to the summer Olympics, Suzanne "Zan" Hagen, an alternate on the U.S. Track Team. Also in the studio is Miss Hagen's coach and friend, schoolboy Arthur Rinehart. Here with them is our resident hostess, Marilyn Bryers. Miss Bryers.

ZAN: *Hola, Mamá. Hola, DumDum,* I mean Walter.

BRYERS (*laughing*): Good morning, Zan. Would you care to say hello in Spanish to anyone else in our audience? Zan's practicing to be an international good neighbor as well as being the internationally ranked runner she is now.

ZAN: *Hola, Señora Tunis.* Hmm—wish you were coming on my trip to L.A. It's not all that far away.

RINEHART: Miss Bryers, may I say, "Please give Zan a passing grade on the test she's missing," to Zan's favorite Spanish teacher?

BRYERS: We haven't time. In an hour Zan will be connecting with a flight to Los Angeles to join her team preparing for its race—the first women's Olympic marathon. Zan, a chief reason I'm pleased to have you here is that you're the one person in Virginia who can answer knowledgeably a question that's been teasing me. What does an alternate do?

ZAN: *No pierde la calma.*

RINEHART: Three Americans will run in the marathon. If one of them is injured or for any reason decides not to run before the race begins, Zan takes her place.

BRYERS: I understand from your coach that you've led a highly active life as an athlete, Zan. You must find it difficult to resign yourself to bench-warming in Los Angeles.

RINEHART: She's doing no such thing. She'll march in the opening ceremonies.

BRYERS: Oh, how colorful! And I wouldn't be surprised if being involved in the controversies surrounding the Olympics also makes your stay in Los Angeles a rewarding one, Zan. You've been following the turmoil over professionalism versus 'shameteurism' on the soccer teams? Have you ever been given money "under the table"?

ZAN: *Ningún peso debajo de nada.*

BRYERS: I see, yes; then moving right along to drug testing—

RINEHART: For the record, ninety-five drugs are banned internationally. Zan has taken only one of them during her training, the caffeine in Pepsi-Cola. But not enough to show up in urine samples.

BRYERS: If Zan participates for America—and our little family here at Channel 7 surely hopes she'll be doing so, Coach Rinehart—might she be at an unfair disadvantage without the amphetamines and steroids reportedly used by distance runners from Iron Curtain countries?

RINEHART: Two of our marathoners are in perfect health and the third seems to have recovered from a muscle pull. Zan *won't* race unless—

ZAN (*blurting*): Unless somebody drives out there and runs over Brown or Benoit or Number Three, DumDum says. He doesn't have a driver's license so he can't do it, don't worry. Hmm. Maybe Mrs. Tunis could. She has this new—

BRYERS: Er, thank you, Zan. Turning to a more nearly positive aspect of being an alternate: Are you excited about your stay in Olympic Village? Meeting members of the track-and-field team. Your teammates?

RINEHART: Our team is still in training in Santa Barbara. Members won't be living in the Village until the opening ceremonies on Saturday.

BRYERS: Then the remainder of this week Zan will have

the opportunity to make friends with athletes from other nations, will she not?

ZAN: Opponents are enemies. I mean *enemigos.*

RINEHART: Zan's trying to explain that she'll be on *my* schedule every minute she's in L.A. She'll be learning the course firsthand by running it. She'll be eating, sleeping, stretching, keeping as fit as she is at present on the remote chance that she'll race.

BRYERS: In that event, Coach, would you care to comment on your strategy for Zan?

RINEHART: No, not in detail. Broadly speaking, she'll stay in contact with the leaders and use my experimental technique for finishing in the pack.

ZAN: Rinehart has this new law: Might's right.

BRYERS: Clearly, Zan, you're going to Los Angeles to win for our country should you be called upon by unforeseen events to compete. For the time being, those on our sports desk are predicting the Eastern European teams will be contenders, and naturally Grete Waitz seems a shoo-in for gold after her first place in Helsinki at the World Championships. Would you care to hazard a guess about the Chinese girl? We've thrilled to her world record from afar.

RINEHART: All we know for certain of Song Mai is that she has run various three-hour marathons in cities like Tokyo and Hong Kong, where her times can be confirmed. Her supposed world record was run behind the bamboo curtain and may be only propaganda to psych us out.

BRYERS: I see that our own time is nearly up—

ZAN: *Hola, Papá.* Wish you and Mom could go to California. *Mírame en la televisión.*

BRYERS: My guest has been an Arlingtonian who now departs for sunny California. Look for this youngster in the opening ceremonies, when ABC Sports begins its coverage of the twenty-third Olympiad. And who knows, during the following week's drama Zan Hagen's face may unexpectedly be in the crowd of women starting their marathon at eleven o'clock Eastern Daylight Savings Time, August 5.

RINEHART: Ask me what the odds are.

# 15

Right away Zan liked Los Angeles. There weren't tons of movie stars in the airport to brag about to Ruby Jean, and outside, the air was the same thick yellow color Rinehart had concocted on his Bunsen burner for Zan to practice breathing. But everything else in L.A. was like the movies. Zan's red, white, and blue shuttle bus whisked her free to Olympic Village, and her room there was air-conditioned and close to a practice track. No roommate had arrived as yet; she was probably still up in Santa Barbara at the team training site. So Zan could choose the top drawer of a bureau to lay her uniforms flat in. Plus the bounciest bed for a nap. Later she pinned her identification tags to her sweat shirt and went in search of food.

Prowling the halls, Zan noticed that on every dorm-room door were two names typed on white cards: her teammates. She should recognize famous sprinters, high jumpers, discus throwers, heptathletes, but she didn't. Zan hadn't followed the track-and-field scene this year. She'd left it to Rinehart and DumDum. The only run-ners she knew by name were the national and inter-national marathoners. Maybe she'd bump into some of these in the dining room she must be coming nearer, for now Zan heard a mob downstairs, across an open court-yard—hundreds of athletes, men and women speaking dozens of languages as they walked through food lines in a dining room the size of a gym.

"Pizza," Zan ordered in fluent Italian when she arrived at the steam table.

"Dos tacos," she ordered, moving along the line.

"Chow mein. Milk. Real orange juice—unfrozen." As much as Zan wanted. She felt greedy until she saw, at the table she chose that everybody's plate was piled higher than hers. She couldn't understand a word her dinner companions said to one another and she didn't give a darn. These were just some enemies from coun-tries the United States had to beat. The girl next to Zan spoke English well enough to startle her with, "You are Californian?"

"No."

"We are volleyballers. You are, too?"

"I'm nothing. A bench jockey." When the listeners didn't seem to understand, Zan added, "I'm a runner."

"Ah, a runner of great distance?"

Zan supposed the whole tableful was maybe Japanese or Chinese. They were smiling at her in such an unexpectedly sweet way they made Zan wish she could remember nice stuff to tell them, Tunis's ideas from her old history class. But she couldn't think of anything except the swell food. "A great runner of distance," Zan ended up agreeing and, "This chow mein tastes awesome."

"You are running with our Song Mai." This was pronounced "Sung May." It went right over Zan's head.

Zan pretended to understand. She nodded acceptance of comments about Song, and as soon as her plates were empty, she lit out for the track. Practice hours were assigned, country by country, during the day, but in the evenings any old nationality could train. Zan stretched out in the bleachers to let dinner digest. She looked for the countries she'd studied in world history.

So many of them. Relaxed in their form, athletes jogged in twos, threes, and more. Some of them did occasional dance steps in time to music from portable stereos parked along the track's curb. Most joggers wore shirts that gave no clue as to what teams they were on. Zan tried to single out the scariest ones on the track, those who'd be "faster, higher, stronger" according to the motto on an Olympic program she'd found in her room. That guy's stronger, Zan thought about a guy practicing with his javelin. She's higher, Zan thought when a girl jumped a hurdle in lane 8. But these athletes weren't scary, not even the super-thin women who were obviously distance runners. Why should they scare Zan in their windbreakers, headphones, and—hey—what's this all about? Who's this girl in a pink dress and a cowboy hat posing for photos? Athletes aren't supposed to have long hair clear down to their bottoms. What's Miss Teen Asia doing here?

"She's no longer China's state secret," Zan heard, and more from photographers.

"She's mighty crowd-pleasing. She's this Olympic's Nadia Comaneci."

"Hello, hello," the Nadia girl said, and dipped her cowboy hat over her eyes. She laughed a gay laugh. One of the media microphones backfired like a loudspeaker and let Zan hear, "To boast of my speed is foolish. If I run faster than the world record, there is nothing special about the record. What has passed is past. More interesting is what on next Sunday will come."

Sunday? Hmm. Which race happens next Sunday besides the women's marathon? Zan wondered.

"They say your kick's a pistol with a silencer."

Sparkling laughter.

"*China Sports* reports you were bounding  around Canton almost before you could crawl."

"She's yet to race in the West," drifted from the track to where Zan sat avoiding a cold fact: this girl under the hat must be Song Mai, hahaha. Big deal. Tough on Song.

Song Mai couldn't scare Zan because Zan would be spectating, not running next Sunday.

"Anyway, I could beat her at a moment's notice. What's so hot about such a young girl?" Zan asked no one paying attention to her. All eyes followed Song Mai slip-slapping across the infield grass in straw thongs.

"East meets West," announced a man wearing ABC emblems on his jacket and tie.

Zan ganged up with the athletes and reporters gaping at Song Mai. It seemed an easy way to get herself seen by Rinehart on national TV. At home he'd be taping whatever turned up on his screen from California. "Hi, Rinehart," Zan moved her lips silently. He'd be reading them three thousand miles away!

"Hello, hello. All praise to your many rapid feet in America." With this simple and direct greeting, Song Mai confronted the West. She noticed Zan on the bottom step of the bleachers and approached her. "I have been searching so far and wide for a young sportswoman like you in our village home, my sight is almost worn out."

The ABC man suggested Zan and Song Mai shake hands for the camera and then run side by side to "demonstrate Eastern versus Western styles of running."

"Hi, Rinehart," Zan said immediately into a microphone.

"Rinehart? Hello to you from Song Mai." She pronounced her own name "Sung Mai." She laughed again. "Rinehart? A city? In Rinehart do you live?" Song Mai closed her hand around Zan's and tugged her onto the track.

"Clear lane 1 for China and the United States of America," ordered a voice on the loudspeaker.

Song Mai stepped out of her sandals.

Zan felt awkward—dishonest—about starring on TV with a genuine Olympian and said so. As they swung along, Zan stated in slow English that she herself was nothing but a substitute runner for the United States. She confessed how she'd raced badly at the trials.

"Those who run faster for your team? Are they in good health?"

"They're perfect—and fast." Zan thought she'd better start psyching out Song Mai for the sake of the old U.S.A.

Song Mai ran along, using the word "reversals" about any runner's training, Americans included. She spoke of the "wear and tear" of her own last year and of not knowing if she'd be sound again for the Olympics. Zan followed words like "knee fluids" and "acupuncture" but wasn't eager to hear more about Song's knee wrapped with a dog skin soaked in herbs. Ugh. Worse bandage than Rinehart would invent in his lab.

They ran the track for ABC's feature story about mainland China's first summer Olympics since 1948. Afterward Song Mai got permission from her coach to run back to the United States wing in Olympic Village. Zan could hardly wait to show somebody in California her uniform, even though she wouldn't ever be wearing it.

"Reversals," Song Mai said again. She didn't bring up

the odds against Zan, the way Rinehart had all summer when Zan asked him if she should give up hope of racing. Hmm. Maybe they didn't have odds or percentages —stuff like that—in the People's Republic of China.

"A souvenir of America?" Song Mai asked in Zan's room. "I will trade my sandals for your shirt."

"You mean it? My shirt's all faded."

Song Mai seemed delighted to trade Zan the straw thongs for a well-worn T-shirt with crossed rifles on the front, a leftover from Zan's Military Marathon. "It matches your trademark," said Zan.

"How so?"

"You're a gun with a silencer," Zan remembered. She asked if she could try on the cowboy hat Song Mai had traded for during yesterday's workout. Song Mai tried on Zan's bathrobe. She stepped into Zan's loafers. She tasted Zan's toothpaste from a tube she'd not seen in China. Zan tasted her own toothpaste. Hmm. She'd never really noticed the mint flavor before. Song Mai gave Zan advice about opening the curtains for more light. Zan gave Song a bar of pink soap that matched her dress. They bounced on the two beds. Song Mai bounced higher, even though she flapped her arms less than Zan. "You win," said Zan. Song's win made Zan want to see who could sprint faster, a bench warmer or the world's record-holder in the marathon. They ran out of Zan's room and along the hall, knocking on doors and fleeing before the doors opened. They ran upstairs to other floors, where they had water fights in bathrooms. In the third-floor lounge Zan tampered with a pop machine until it sent two cans of caffeine-free Dr. Pepper out of the slot for nothing. "Fritz Slappy showed me how," she told Song.

"He lives with you in Rinehart?"

"Rinehart's my coach. Fritz is—Fritz is a friend, except I don't have friends when I'm training, and I've been training for the Olympics since last November."

"What is sport unless it brings friendships?"

Zan had to think about it. She thought, Hey, what am I doing here with my country's enemy? My team's enemy? My own personal enemy if I have to race against her on the fifth? She's awesome. Is she really awesome? Zan asked. Zan and Song Mai were running downstairs, tracking the sound of gunshot to the dormitory lobby. There they watched snatches of an old Western on TV.

"This film we have seen in Canton many like it," Song Mai whispered to the other athletes sharing her sofa. She admired the film's horses. She was a city girl in China, she whispered to Zan. She admired the cowboys' boots and jeans. She'd trade her dress and her red bandana and her humblest thank you for a pair of Levi's.

"Swap you my earrings for yours," suggested a woman waiting near the lobby phone booth.

In no time Song Mai had made the trade and was deep in conversation with others in the lobby. Her tone, friendly and courteous, brought everyone closer to the sofa. Her impressive English accompanied her hands and eyes to express the love she had for Canton, that city of her happiest marathon. There people threw flowers in the streets as she ran.

"Were flowers the secret of your world record?" a woman leaned forward to ask.

"Secret? I contain no secret."

"If you confide your training schedule to me it's safe. My sport's field hockey," said a woman in a British accent.

Song Mai gave a quick laugh. "Training schedule?" She tilted her cowboy hat toward the TV screen. "These Western horses run more swiftly than I."

"How many meters do you train every week?"

"As you will." Song Mai smiled, saying, "I run at break of dawn. Evenings also."

"*Combien de mètres?*"

"*Cuantos metros?*"

"I train as our world trains. I sleep at night."

"How many hours?"

"I eat fresh—"

"Do China's distance runners use carbohydrate loading before their races?" asked the British woman, who was by now up in Song Mai's face.

"Loading?" Song Mai seemed sincerely puzzled.

"She eats flowers," Zan filled in. This joke didn't halt questions. To do that Song Mai covered her ears with her hands.

A woman waiting for the phone jingled Song Mai's tiny bell earrings. "There you are. Symbols of the ancient Orient."

"Mystery is still a weapon in their arsenal," Great Britain decided.

"Her best secret's how she runs so fast in a dress," quipped Zan. She wanted these women to stop hassling Song Mai. "China's a nice person, umm, so leave her alone."

But even Zan herself wanted to know the truth about Song's world record and if Song's workouts had been as long and painful as the ones Rinehart invented, and if Song believed she could beat England, France, Italy, New Zealand, and these other countries that were grilling her. Song Mai continued to sit among the curious Olympians. During a break from gunshots on TV, Zan heard her whisper, "We are not mysterious. Our training is for better stride length and form."

Someone turned off the TV.

"In China we try to develop proper racing pace. Our coaches enter us in marathons for much experience."

What pace will you be setting against Julie Brown next Sunday? Zan wished she could ask. She didn't because Song Mai's voice seemed sad as she whispered, "Often I fail my coaches."

Others asked, "Do your coaches believe in blood doping?"

"Or in bionics?"

"Or wonder drugs?"

Zan interrupted. "There's tons of countries running around Olympic Village looking like they jumped out of test tubes." She was trying to change the subject because China seemed to be fading into the sofa.

"Do Chinese athletes use steroids? Are you clean?"

Song Mai must not have understood the question, for she answered, "In Canton we have bathing tubs."

Laughter was followed by a lobby-wide discussion of Olympic drug screening. Zan excused herself, tugged Song Mai by the sash of her dress, and headed for the dining room. At a table next to the dessert bar they ate flavor after flavor of ice cream. Zan identified each of them for Song, saying, "Rice cream," to make her new friend giggle. Song Mai daydreamed aloud about chocolate chips growing in China.

Hanging out, full and relaxed, Zan wondered if China's coaches studied the racing styles of opponents the same way Rinehart had studied Waitz, Mota, Roe—stars who were regularly praised in marathon magazines. Zan had been infected by the questions of others this evening. "Did you ever hear of me before?" she asked Song Mai. "Before now?"

"No. But in future I will hear more of you. You are filled with goodwill."

"You'll change your mind when you feel my finishing shove," Zan threatened with a grin, but immediately realized Song Mai wouldn't feel any Zan Hagen move because Zan Hagen wasn't racing. She shouldn't get her hopes— "Tell me other stuff about reversals," Zan begged Song Mai.

But rather than wait for Song Mai to cheer her up, Zan remembered out loud something goofy Mrs. Tunis had said in class. "My teacher, she thinks everyone in the world should be allowed to run the Olympic marathon. Anyone who wants to. They should just show up at the starting line. Drive there. Fly, catch a boat, even if there's around a million of them, and take off together and go for it when the starter says 'Go.' "

Song Mai loved the notion.

"Mrs. Tunis doesn't believe in starting guns. She says the Olympic marathon ought to start in peace. It should be an event that doesn't need qualifying times. Everyone's qualified for a fun run. Any human could be an Olympian. Plus they all get olive leaves at the finish line!"

"How fine."

"The whole idea stinks. Tunis thought it up to make me feel okay about failing. I stink." Zan pushed aside her ice cream. "*You* don't mind who runs against you or even if you win a medal!"

Song Mai touched her forehead to show where her own training had failed. "China coaches, they try to stiffen my desire to excel. They give many fruitful suggestions. With me their diligence is unrewarded."

"You with your 2:20 world record?"

"Ah, so different from my other races. In Canton's streets I was not alone. I ran for many friends nearby with flowers."

"You're psyching me—you're kidding me." Zan had never heard of anything so silly.

She sat there and thought about it in the warmth of Song Mai's encouraging words about reversals. Zan was lulled into her own memory of how lonely running and racing had often been for her. She recalled her Lee pals and other friendly people who'd helped her along the course in Durham. And how about thoughtful Julie

Brown, who'd tried to help her in Olympia? Maybe if Coach Rinehart had been standing at the 26-mile mark hollering "Zanbanger" and throwing firecrackers she might have shoved her way to third.

Friends mattered a lot. Zan admitted it.

She began trading stories with Song Mai of their past races. They swapped reasons for running in the Olympics: Zan's to be "best," a whole page in sports history books; Song Mai's to please her many friends at home. After a while their feet itched to run. "Let's race out of here," Zan said. Song Mai pointed her hat west at a window. "Outside. Our marathon path."

"You'll need shoes. Come on upstairs."

They raced back to Zan's room. Zan won by holding her hands on each side of the stair railings to force Song Mai behind. Once in the room, Song Mai tried on Zan's Adidas. She looked super in blue, Zan said, and offered her a set of blue, white, and red sweats.

"My coaches would not be happy to see me on your American team."

Zan answered, "They can't see in the dark."

Los Angeles darkness presented no problem to Song Mai. In no time she'd guided Zan to the powder-blue line that ran down the middle of every street, avenue, boulevard, freeway, and road of their Olympic course.


Blue shoes on the blue line. Song Mai and Zan were running forward but backward on the course toward

Santa Monica. Rinehart would have a fit if he saw Zan. He'd spent so many evenings leading her feet straight ahead over this course in his laboratory, where, on the floor, he'd chalked a map in blue.

Let him have a fit, Zan thought. Caresies! Tonight she was running for fun for a change. She could grin when Song Mai welcomed people strolling in their way. She could join Song Mai's "Hello, hello" to these three women running directly toward them on the line.

In unison Zan and Song sidestepped. It was that or fall down under the weight of East Germany.

"I've seen them in photos. They stick together, move mechanically. They don't mean well," Zan told her friend. "They run against you as a team. They box. They crowd you."

Song Mai had already doffed her hat.

"Hey, you'll waste them next Sunday, I hope I hope."

"I have hope you then will run with me."

Song Mai's hope made Zan jump a fire plug. Tonight she wanted to mess around, stay out until daylight, eat fifty waffles for breakfast—except Song Mai would for sure be competing. She had better return Song to her China roommates for bed check. "Giddap," coached Zan. Back in the lobby she said, "Night" to her new best friend in California. Then Zan claimed an easy chair for the late movie.

Rinehart would be in shock if he knew she stayed up for nothing but fun. Not until 5:00 a.m. Arlington time did Zan go upstairs. She banged open the door of her room to see the third-place winner at the trials asleep in the room's other bed. Zan's own bed had a slip of stationery tucked beside the pillow but she missed seeing it in her speed to dream of competing with Song Mai.

# 16

California sunshine. It showed Zan the handwritten note from distance-running coach Doris Heritage asking could they meet for breakfast Friday.

Not unless breakfast was still being served in the mid-afternoon.

A further message, stuck in the mirror, invited Zan to march along with her roommate tomorrow in opening ceremonies. Okay, Zan would. Marching inside the Los Angeles Coliseum would give her a chance to test the Olympic track. She knew from Rinehart that it was polyurethane covering five inches of crushed rock. He'd said it would be springy, a surface designed to store up runners' energy and return it to them each step. Just too darn bad the entire twenty-six miles weren't being run on such a trampoline of a track.

Officially Zan wouldn't be racing one step of those twenty-six miles. *Unofficially* she might try to sneak along the course and use her shove to keep enemies from crowding the leader, Song Mai. Zan hoped Song Mai would lead from the start in Santa Monica. And if friendly people threw orange blossoms at her, she might put out the effort to hold her lead. Zan herself could scatter coconuts from palm trees in front of Song Mai. That would be more fun than hanging idly on a curb watching the race.

Hanging around. Watching. Not competing. Alone in her room, Zan cried her eyes out.

Her tears put her back to sleep. Being a substitute had caught up with Zan in California.

Reawakening in twilight, Zan realized she'd slept the day away. So what? She didn't need to train. She could see from her bed that her roommate wasn't there. Her clothes were, in a neat pile, and a stack of postcards on the bureau, bottles of pills, a can of hairspray, and a Whitman's Sampler.

Zan got up and ate a gold-wrapped chocolate from the top layer.

Let's go back to the pills, she thought. She read directions on the bottles. She uncapped a bottle marked *For pain only*. She sniffed the contents and immediately wiped her nose. She snatched her towel and rushed for the shower. Whew! She didn't want steroid whiskers, not unless she was racing *officially*.

Again in her room, Zan took charge of herself. "Eat dinner," she coached. "Go back in training." Her rituals would keep her mind and body from slouching in sorrow. "Pretend you're at home on the road. Home players have the advantage," Rinehart had taught her. "Maintain your usual rhythms, as if you were in Arlington."

Zan ate dinner in a babel of languages. She wished she'd taken a class in Albanian instead of Spanish. "Asspay the alt-say," she muttered. She left the dining room without dessert. She rode a bus from Olympic Village to Exposition Park and did her speed drills in a rose garden. Tomorrow these grounds would be jammed for opening ceremonies. Inside the Coliseum there'd be 92,000 sports fans. Out here, double that number trying by hook or crook to peer at the track inside. Then on Sunday, the fifth of August, another audience of thousands would see women marathoners finish their race by entering the Coliseum through a tunnel Zan now approached.

Guards wouldn't let her through the west gate.

Hmm. The tunnel appeared at a distance to be about fifty yards long, dark and probably cold. It seemed more fearful than the tunnel Rinehart had scouted out for Zan to practice in. He'd considered every inch of her Olympic marathon course. He'd sent Zan to Maryland in Monk's car to practice in a train tunnel. Rinehart wanted her to get accustomed to eerie footfalls and the chilling air after twenty-six miles of running in sun.

Tonight Zan looked down the Coliseum tunnel longingly. She'd give anything to be racing through it on the fifth. Oh, the pain.

"Back off," a guard barked.

"This is no place for children," another guard said gently.

"I'm marching through here tomorrow, fellows. At opening ceremonies." So saying, Zan ran home to bed again.

She didn't dream. Even in sleep she understood the odds against her racing. Reversals? They were Oriental mumbo-jumbo.

Saturday morning Zan finally met her roommate, the third-place American girl. Zan thought she looked pale for someone who'd been training in California all summer. Zan called her "Three" and "Eee-thray" when they spoke, which was twice. Later they assembled with the entire United States team in the Coliseum parking lot. As the host country they'd be last to march through the tunnel, into the stadium, and around the 400-meter track. Zan had waiting time enough to snap the waistband on her warm-up suit so often it loosened. She also had ample opportunity to avoid Number Three.

National anthems wafted from the Coliseum, one after another. Zan tried to make out which one was China's, but they all sounded alike, including the "Star-Spangled Banner," when it was played at long last.

"Let's march. Left, right." Captains sent their teams across the parking lot.

"What so proudly we hail."

"Hail."

"Hail," sang voices out of sync around Zan. A tall American Indian girl led the U.S. Track and Field Team.

"Left, right, left, right," captains hollered. Some athletes were strutting, jumping, skipping on any old foot like a bunch of individuals. At Zan's side Number Three kept pace for twenty yards. Then, entering the tunnel, she slowed. Zan automatically moved ahead, but after a few steps she dropped off with Number Three, and soon they both were well behind their teammates.

Number Three leaned against the tunnel wall.

"Our guys are out on the track already," Zan bawled at her. "Get it together."

The tunnel echoed, "Together."

Number Three slithered down the wall to a seated position. She wrapped her arms around her stomach and moaned, "My leg."

"What are you talking about? You weren't limping bad. Come on." All Zan could think of was that Rine-hart and her mom and dad and DumDum and probably Mrs. Tunis would be missing her on ABC Sports if she didn't wave from the Coliseum track, wave and say, "I love you, everybody."

"I'm fine. Catch up with the others, Suzanne," Number Three said, too soft for an echo.

"It's icky here. Damp. I can't leave you alone." Zan didn't really know what the heck she was saying. She couldn't care less about this lame wimp on the tunnel floor.

Lifting herself to her feet again, Number Three murmured, "I'm after my pills." She struggled backward, toward the parking lot.

"Save your leg for the marathon. I'll go get your drugs."

Zan couldn't believe she'd said it. She took three strides up the tunnel, turned around, took three strides down to roll her jacket into a pillow for Number Three.

"This isn't happening. It can't be," Zan said half aloud.

She thought if she hotfooted it to the Olympic Village she could be back in time to search the grandstands for the fruitcake. She wanted to see any old friend, even F. Parnell Manfred. Zan felt homesick. She felt sick, period, about missing the parade.

Meeting a guard at the tunnel's entrance, Zan pointed back to the dark. "Fix that girl up while I'm gone— she's on our marathon team. I'll get the medicine. I can run faster than her."

# 17

"You're faster than a speed-ing bullet," Zan told Song Mai.

Together they'd burst from the starting line practi-cally on top of seventy other runners. The first women's Olympic marathon was underway, and every competitor raced the track at Santa Monica College as if she'd been stuffed in the muzzle of a gun these eighty-eight years since the original Olympic marathon for men.

1896–1984.

August 5.

8:00 a.m., California time.

Aimed at the Coliseum on a roundabout course of twenty-six miles through Los Angeles.

Fired.

Right from the start Zan used her Rinehart shove. Whichever nation chanced to be near her left elbow caught a dig in the ribs. And plenty more later, as Zan followed Rinehart's new plan. Within the tight pack of marathoners her mayhem went unnoticed from the bleachers.

"Gotcha," chortled Zan to Rumiko Kaneko on her left. "Take that, Japan."

"Hello, hello." Song Mai kissed her palms and reached to touch an armed guard at the track's north gate. Runners were squeezing through this narrow opening onto 17th Street in Santa Monica.

Song Mai and Zan swapped playful elbows. They ran north on 17th Street in a large pack that just didn't thin out. It moved along behind press trucks burping gas. It moved between two long columns of motorcycle policemen wearing riot guns slung over their backs. This escort shouted, "Remain on sidewalks," to the crowd.

Zan hoped that anyone throwing flowers wouldn't be bumped off by these fierce-looking police all in black. Their motors drowned the footsteps and breathing of runners behind her. Hmm. How close to her shoulder were other countries running now?

Crossing Santa Monica Freeway on the overpass, Zan decided to count the front-running women. "Sixteen ahead on Olympic Boulevard," Zan said to Song Mai.

"I will fare better not to hear numbers we must pass."

Zan eyed Song Mai for a facial expression other than a spreading smile. She wanted a clue to Song's strategy.

Didn't it matter to China's race plan if Grete Waitz and others were leading?

I can't help her plan, Zan warned herself. I'm in THE OLYMPICS. China's our enemy, best friend or not.

But despite her self-warning, Zan whispered, "Julie Brown's on your right, and Brown means business."

"Hello, hello, Julie. Those who run beyond you test your wondrous speed."

Julie Brown clipped past to take her place among the front-runners. Zan and Song Mai settled with this pack into a steady pace. They ran up a sharp hill, which in one hundred yards would meet Wilshire Boulevard. There they all turned east to be glared at by morning sun rays bouncing off shop windows. Zan griped about the heat. She asked Song Mai to keep an eye out for Arthur Rinehart at a water station. It would be just like him to bamboozle Olympic officials and help them hand out cups and sponges. "You burning up yet, Song Mai?"

"Feel the ocean wind."

Now that Song Mai mentioned it, Zan noticed wind blowing at their backs from the Pacific. "Thanks a lot," she responded. Cooled, Zan could wander off into memories of all the good times she'd had since arriving in California.

What fun! Ten days of it. Hanging out with Song Mai took first place—took the gold for happy memories. In second place was phoning Mr. Manfred at the Beverly Hills Hotel. She'd missed seeing him in the Coliseum during opening ceremonies. It had taken Zan too long to chase down bottles of pills, and then Zan couldn't find

Number Three, who'd been carried to a first-aid station in Exposition Park. Number Three's hamstring had killed her all summer. She'd become hooked on pain pills and wound up pretending she felt fine in order to stay on the United States team. When Zan phoned Rinehart collect and explained how she'd be racing in the Olympics after all, he'd promised to scheme up a free car ride to California for himself.

Hearing Rinehart's astonished voice on the phone—the first time in his whole life he didn't know it all—was Zan's bronze medal for fun in California.

She thought about him as she and Song Mai drifted left onto Bundy Drive. Zan heard Rinehart's voice all the way from his lab saying, "Bundy's uphill." But Zan couldn't feel the incline, not in her leg muscles, not in her lungs. She ran comfortably just twenty yards behind the lead pack.

"These houses are like yours?" Song Mai broke into Zan's memories. Song meant the mansions lining Bundy Drive, and no, they weren't like the Hagen house in Arlington. "Ours are much littler. We don't have these flowery yards," Zan admitted.

"Ah, true?" Song Mai continued to swing her head left and right, gazing at the scenery. Because of their fun runs all week, Zan was used to Song's wasting energy like that. Zan herself stared straight ahead at the course until she heard:

"Boyohboyohboy. Lemme through here. How 'bout that?"

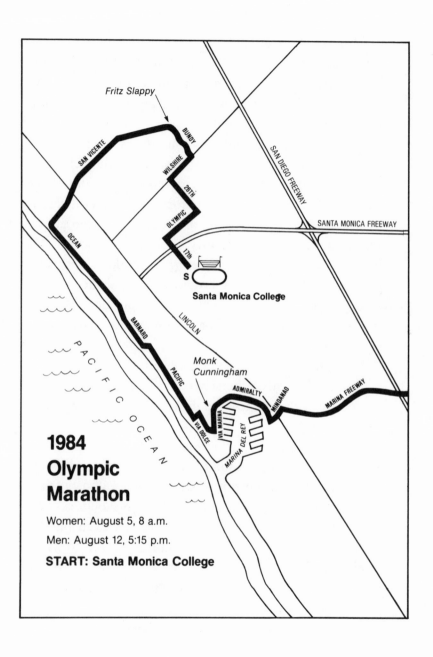

Fritz Slappy

SAN VICENTE

BUNDY

WILSHIRE

26TH

OLYMPIC

OCEAN

17th

S

Santa Monica College

SAN DIEGO FREEWAY

SANTA MONICA FREEWAY

BARNARD

LINCOLN

PACIFIC

Monk Cunningham

ADMIRALTY

MINDANAO

MARINA FREEWAY

VIA MARINA

VIA DOLCE

MARINA DEL REY

PACIFIC OCEAN

**1984 Olympic Marathon**

Women: August 5, 8 a.m.

Men: August 12, 5:15 p.m.

**START: Santa Monica College**

Motorcycles were coasting quietly around the corner onto San Vicente Boulevard, so Zan heard Fritz Slappy hollering at her plain as day. She looked for him on the sidewalks behind barricades. He'd be wearing a white sailor suit, she remembered.

"Way to fly, Zan. Ditto all you other suckers."

There Fritz stood, thumbing his nose at the field. Zan spent some of her precious energy pointing at him. Song Mai said, "Handsome man," before a helicopter directly overhead made it impossible to speak. It hovered above the front-runners all their way west on San Vicente. Its blade provided a breeze. Trees growing down the very middle of the boulevard provided some shade. NAKED CORAL TREES, Zan read on a low bronze plaque she'd seen while making sure her shoes were pointed absolutely forward.

Underfoot were fallen coral blossoms.

Zan tried to make herself heard over the helicopter engine. "Check out these red flowers," she called to Song Mai.

Then Zan shut up. She'd thought better of helping her friend. They now sped south on Ocean Boulevard. Song Mai's eyes strayed far out to sea, picking sailboats from morning fog. Zan's eyes studied her own shoelaces, tied in so many knots they'd never untie, not even on the Coliseum victory stand, where Zan had figured to slam-dunk her shoes. All was well for the four-mile stretch atop Santa Monica Palisades, through Venice, and into Marina del Rey.

All except there was no trace of Rinehart.

Song Mai would probably see him first. Still fresh and bubbly after eleven miles, she cheered the spectators and gave them an occasional wave if someone read PRC out loud from her singlet. Song Mai knew exactly what Rinehart looked like. She'd heard about his dippy steel-rimmed glasses and about the notebook he clamped between his teeth when he hand-signaled Zan for the Rinehart Kick and Shove. Poor Song Mai! On their training runs this past week, she'd listened endlessly to Zan talk about her coach.

Twelve miles and no Rinehart.

They ran the Gran Corso Bridge.

Then Via Dolce. The original tight pack of twenty women had long since strung out one hundred yards into smaller packs. Zan and Song Mai remained with Ireland and Canada. This foursome approached the 180-degree turn at Bora Bora Way. Ahead of them, actually coming toward them on the other side of Admiralty Way, were three Russians, Grete Waitz, and Julie Brown. They were followed in ten yards by three East Germans glued to two West Germans. Song Mai shouted a word of praise to all these leaders: "Formidable!"

"Op-dray ed-day," Zan chimed in.

She was answered by Monk Cunningham overhead in a palm tree. Zan spotted him all red-faced from clinging to the trunk. Who else would be singing "God Bless America" to her with the words in Spanish. Zan had no greeting for Monk. He'd understand she was saving her breath for the victory stand.

Coming up on the 13.1 marker, Zan was wondering if

she ought to start putting some moves on Song Mai. Try to psych her out with comments. Or with speed? Try to take over the lead and blow away these foreign countries instead of just staying in contact with them, watching them and waiting for signs they were tiring. Maybe Zan should start thinking about Rinehart's race plan, which didn't include enjoying the company of an enemy. "Let's go easy here," Zan told Song Mai. They clicked into a lower gear in response to the front-running pack.

Plenty of miles left for Zan to make moves.

# 18

A marathon footrace is a series of small events:

### Mile 13.3

Zan noticed facial hair. Finally! Her nationwide search brought her almost cheek to whiskery cheek with an Albanian runner wedging between her and Song Mai.

### Mile 14.6

A kid jumped off a fire hydrant on Mindanao Way, wriggled between two motorcycles, lunged at Ireland, ripped off her race number, screamed "I.R.A. forever," knifed through the sidewalk crowd, and disappeared. Ireland's Cary May scarcely broke her stride. She didn't answer Zan's offer to chase the kid down after their race.

## Mile 16.1

Route 90, the Marina Freeway, took its toll of front-runners. Belyayeva (Russia) was hanging on a guard rail when Zan and Song Mai chugged past. Vahlensieck (West Germany) stood blowing her nose and coughing. Must be the fumes from all these mufflers, Zan thought. Her own throat felt smooth because she still held gulps of water in her mouth from the last aid station. She swallowed a drop every quarter mile, playing Rinehart's game with herself to pass the time up a cement hill.

## 17.1

One more mile on the freeway: Zan's eyes had been smarting until a sudden hot wind swirled the dense carbon monoxide away.

## 17.3

Runners toiled east into the climbing sun. Zan placed herself closer to Song Mai's left elbow. Albania, fading, couldn't come between them. "Don't get so near me, Bluebeard, I haven't brushed my teeth this morning," she warned the Albanian gruffly. "Higher, faster, stronger, meaner," Zan whispered her new Olympic motto to Song Mai.

### 17.5

The temperature rose along their blue line. "Maybe it's eighty-five degrees?" Zan asked Song Mai. Close to them New Zealand's knees buckled. Zan didn't glance behind at the body. Neither did Song Mai.

### 17.8–18.2

Local residents in front yards were shading their eyes, looking up at a trail of vapor from a skywriter:

LEE HIGH RUNS WITH ZAN

Zan missed this surprise psych-up in the sky. On her twisting course from Slauson to Hannum to Playa she had no reserve strength to waste tipping her head back to check out the Goodyear blimp, the jet fighters, and whatever else happened to be up there now. Nor did Song Mai see the tribute to Lee's favorite athlete. Song had dropped behind Zan at the Marina Freeway ramp.

### 18.8

Fifty yards north of where Zan now ran on Overland the lead was changing. Zan said to Song Mai, "East Germany's coming back to us, one of them."

Mexico ran at Zan's side in place of Song Mai.

Zan asked Mexico, "Where's China?"

Marialuisa Ronquillo answered something that sounded like "Gasp."

"*Por favor, Donde está la República Popular de Chino?*" Zan spoke her summer-school Spanish. Then she added, "I'm giving you from here to that American flag on the curb to answer my question or you'll get elbowed from Overland to Disneyland."

19

Rather than shove anyone, Zan glanced over her shoulder for Song Mai. She couldn't see through Portugal's Rosa Mota running directly behind. So Zan stopped. She turned around and saw a fluttering American flag and none other than F. Parnell Manfred under it. Zan dashed back to him. She hollered, "Throw your flag at a Chinese girl all in red with long black hair down to here when she runs past you."

"Is she part of your wonderful team, Suzanne?"

"She People's Republic—P.R.C."

Manfred draped Zan in his flag.

"You total fru—Okay, here." Zan pulled green shoots from a bushy tree. "Throw these at China. Look for the pink flowers I drew around her race number. Got that? She's helping me win, hear? She's my new race plan."

19

Zan set out to recover her lost time. She fled past Joyce Smith (Great Britain).

### 19.1

She passed weeping Belgium, who was sidesaddle on a parked motorcycle.

### 19.2

She caught Rosa Mota.

### 19.3

At least once every block on Jefferson Boulevard Zan looked back. How can I be doing this, Zan thought, looking back. She missed her Chinese friend at her side.

### 19.4

Zan felt lonely. The next runners she caught up with, she'd try to speak their languages.

### 19.5

Another helicopter and an ambulance drowned laughter from the deepening crowd as it watched a stark-naked streaker on the marathon course. The streaker didn't even wear a number.

### 19.6

Clinging to the streaker's bare heels, Zan wondered if the helicopter had a camera and if Rinehart, who must be still home in Arlington, was taping Zan's X-rated marathon on his Betamax.

### 19.7

The streaker had a tattoo that Zan tried to read as she outstreaked him.

### 19.8

Zan couldn't have heard a tidal wave behind her in the commotion of police cars. Cops must be throwing the streaker into a paddy wagon.

### 19.9

But Zan heard and recognized Adidas footsteps, the same cadence she'd been listening to during her after-dinner fun runs for the past week: light steps, quickly taken by Song Mai.

# 19

They must be doing something right. Zan and Song Mai ran up there with the leaders. Together they held the blue marathon line behind a cluster of women around Norway's Grete Waitz. Grete's pace had been slow for twenty miles, just as Rinehart had predicted. This would be a tactical race, not an attempt by anyone to set a world record. Winning the gold was all that mattered. Who cared how fast?

Unless Song Mai secretly planned to kiss the pack goodbye soon and pour it on for a convincing 2:20 this side of the Pacific.

Even if Song Mai broke away, Zan believed the rest of the leaders would stay with Grete's pace judgment, for wasn't she the world's greatest woman marathoner ever? You bet, the greatest on page after page of Rinehart's Log.

"Norway's bound to show us her race plan soon," Zan said to Song Mai.

"We have much left in our legs."

"Back there—did some guy in a Hawaiian shirt throw leaves at you, huh? A few miles ago?" Zan reached over to pluck a leaf from Song Mai's hair, still dry after twenty-one miles.

"A gentleman of goodwill."

Zan didn't correct her friend.

"His kindness prevails. Make now a clean break, we two."

What was Song Mai up to with her swifter pace?

Who should Zan trust this morning? A kid who ran a mythical world record for her flower-throwing friends' sake? Or the twenty-nine-year-old winner of five New York City marathons?

Zan muttered, "I'm staying in the pack with Norway."

Song opened her stride, yet her gaiety was unaffected by the faster pace. Zan lay back and watched China pat and pass a Russian, pat Laura Fogli, the only Italian remaining among front-runners—pat Fogli and scoot in front of her. Zan thought, What fun! There were two and a half billion fans around the world watching this super TV treat: the People's Republic of China now whistling between East and West Germany.

It would be even more fun if I hustled on ahead with

Song Mai, Zan continued thinking. We'll build up a lead on Queen-of-the-Roads Waitz. She'll never overcome us. Zan took her pace up a notch while deciding. She felt comfortable. Then up, up in another gear she cut the gap between her and Song Mai to two yards, one yard— " 'Lo, China," Zan said, nothing else. At this speed they'd have to let their actions do the speaking.

They ran as they felt, and they felt fine for a mile on Rodeo Road. They passed Julie Brown. They passed Waitz. They didn't slack off when they found themselves the front-runners, either. They both drew strength from the crowd's electricity. Zan was certain she heard DumDum yelling at her from atop a car stopped at an intersection. Who else would notice her nose running, caused by a swig of water that seemed to be going up, not down, her throat?

Speed makes the body act strangely, Zan knew from experience.

"Hagen, lookit, you're leaking."

Zan sweat on the blue line.

Then a gust of Santa Ana wind dried her sweat into salt patches on her face. These cracked with each knee lift. Thinking also made her face crack into a grin. If DumDum's around L.A., Zan thought, Rinehart's here. DumDum couldn't have found his way to California all alone.

Coach Rinehart, check me out with China in first place, Zan wished she could shout to him wherever he lurked in the crowd.

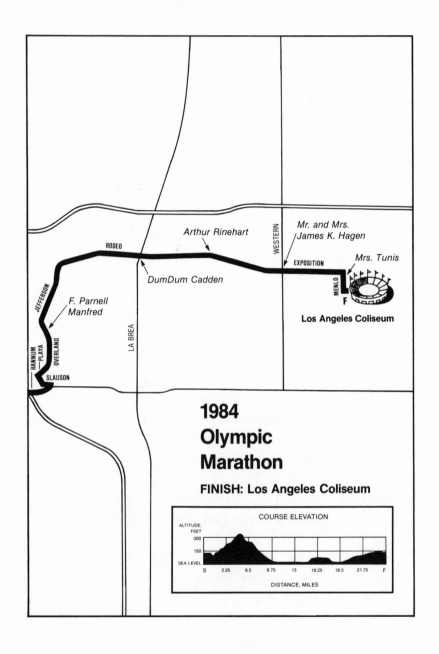

Arthur Rinehart

Mr. and Mrs.
James K. Hagen

WESTERN

EXPOSITION

Mrs. Tunis

RODEO

DumDum Cadden

JEFFERSON

F. Parnell
Manfred

LA BREA

OVERLAND

HANNUM
PLAYA

SLAUSON

MENLO

F

**Los Angeles Coliseum**

# 1984
# Olympic
# Marathon

## FINISH: Los Angeles Coliseum

COURSE ELEVATION

ALTITUDE,
FEET

300

150

SEA LEVEL

S   3.25   6.5   9.75   13   16.25   18.5   21.75   F

DISTANCE, MILES

She'd already used her shouting breath on speed.

Their pace sure didn't seem to bother Song Mai. A sidelong glance at her convinced Zan she was running with a flower that didn't wilt no matter what. They sped directly behind the pace car with its giant Seiko clock at

2:00:00

Smog from that car, from press trucks and motor-cycles clouded Zan's vision, which had already lessened under stress. She could see Song Mai's uniform fresh as a rose. But Zan could barely see beyond her friend to the noisemakers screaming:

"Go get her, America."

"You're stoked."

"Way to be, U.S.A."

"Make them eat your dust and thunder."

Rinehart's very words. Zan strained to sort his signals from the tangle of hands lining Rodeo Road.

Oh, heck, what did she need with the Rinehart shove? She wouldn't elbow China, not at this speed. Zan wanted a runner right beside her at this mile in the race, a body to pull her along. Plus Zan wouldn't hurt another country in plain view. Not in front of cameras from every newspaper and magazine in the world.

"Your—coach—shakes—his—book." Song Mai sounded winded, like Julie Brown at the trials.

"He's—proud—of—us." Zan couldn't bring herself to quote Rinehart's actual message.

With his shaking Log he'd signaled her to do anything in the next three miles for a gold. He'd said it's win at any cost. It's do or die, kill or be killed. Zan must fluff off the world by any means and retain the lead, or else crawl home to Virginia in the shame of silver or bronze or fourth or seventieth or DNF.

They were both deep in oxygen debt, Zan and Song Mai. Zan realized how deep from her own troubled lungs and from Song Mai's breathy efforts at words. They were talking to themselves in these final precious minutes of the marathon. Zan begged herself "Do——it," but this measly psych-up didn't keep her body from caving in. Her joints protested with each jolting step down Exposition Boulevard. Her last drink of water, torn from an aid station, had given her a side stitch.

Did Song Mai feel as close as Zan did to dropping dead?

Ask her, Zan thought.

She won't tell me.

Test her by slowing.

They gave up their sprint simultaneously. Neither said why. Zan swiped her eyes with a fist, squinted, and saw the Coliseum ahead on the right. It gleamed white.

It stayed far in the distance and it wavered.

The marathon line wavered. Blue paint seemed to flow into glazed pools underfoot.

Dream steps on this dream boulevard. Only her mind kept Zan from falling behind the slowing China. From falling, period. Zan dreamed of Frank Shorter's gins.

She'd go him one better by drinking a quart of them after this everlasting race. She'd gobble more chocolate than Spiridon Louis did in 1896—starting with both layers of the Whitman's Sampler that Isabelle Carmichael had given her for delivering her pain-killing pills to Exposition Park.

"Right. Right."

Zan heard a dream voice. She dream-felt an elbow nudging her into a right turn at yet another street in Exposition Park. Zan's Jell-O legs turned the corner. Her dreamy mind stayed on old Dorando Pietri. He must have felt this exhausted when he collapsed in the stadium. He must have felt surprised by the helping hands. Hands that got him disqualified! Zan came to her senses thinking, would she be disqualified at the finish line for accepting a helping elbow from Song Mai?

Maybe no one saw them.

Are you out of your mind? Zan thought. They ran along the Coliseum's west side in full view of the entire TV-watching population of the United States of America. People screamed out Zan's race number from lamp poles and trees, from seats on the curb and each other's shoulders. They'd learned her name, the ones with Olympic programs. Zan ran down a corridor of "H-A-G-E-N."

Never mind that. Zan felt she was sinking.

"Turn left."

Zan let Song Mai command them into a 180-degree turn toward Westgate of the Coliseum. Together they leaned left, left, left, until they could see racers no more than fifteen yards behind them on the course, women kicking like broncos. Waitz's blond ponytail sailed out behind her. Two East Germans bared their teeth. Oh oh.

The moment had arrived for the kick part of Rinehart's Kick and Shove, Zan knew without his signals to coach her. "Dig deeper," she wheezed to herself. She moved from dying to kicking without going through her other gears in between. She charged the Coliseum gate. She entered the musty tunnel. She coasted down an unremembered slope.

Light bulbs twinkled on the tunnel walls.

Footfalls echoed behind Zan in the dank air, unrecognizable footfalls.

Zan looked backward for Song Mai and saw her lying on the tunnel floor. Zan looked forward toward the comfy track at the bottom of this narrowing tunnel. Two voices yelled *"Rasch"* in Zan's ear.

Zan wasn't about to *rasch* or anything else in East German. They never passed me, never will, she thought, and suddenly got collared, got sandwiched between two —two rotten onions, smelled like. Didn't anyone brush teeth before a race?

It's shove time. No one could see Zan in the tunnel using her finely trained arms to send two onions reeling to the concrete. Zan turned around, sprang uphill, grabbed Song Mai by her wrists, set her on her feet, and pointed to a bend at the tunnel's end. "Green grass," Zan gasped. "Trade you grass for—"

They pressed down their shoes. They fled for the Coliseum's sunlight. They smelled infield grass as they jumped a short curb to the track.

Red, bouncy track. It caught their feet and gave them back quickly. Zan stayed with Song's pace, but they both knew they'd be caught from behind if they didn't blaze this final lap.

What to do, what to do, Zan thought. Song's too tired to run faster.

Zan took Song Mai's hand there in front of the world. Let any old nationality watch her help her teammate China, and watch China help her. Let them watch their eyes out, okay, and cheer for disqualification. We don't care. Zan looked down the straightaway to the finish line. Is that all there is? she thought.

Then didn't think. She felt. She felt their swinging hands cross the finish line together.